The Alien Kore Threat

© Copyright 2011

By Earl Lacy

All Rights Reserved

ISBN 13: 987-0997085655
ISBN 10: 0997085657

Printed in the United States.

By: Ecclesia Publishing House LLC
ecclesiaph@gmail.com

Table of Contents

They fled from justice in the Centaurus Constellation: Criminals, Terrorists, Murders, plus a Serial Killer--- led by Alien Kore, arrived on Earth to conquer and declare himself the System Lord! But after a devastation war, Kore was defeated yet escaped. Years later, Kore returned with a monumental wrath and a new more vicious ally.

CHAPTER ONE
THE CONFLICT

The Centaurus Empire was 17,000 light years from Earth. It was a federation of planets united under one leader, Sri Kordova, a wise System Lord.

As with all intelligent species, there arose serious disagreements that couldn't be resolved with a treaty followed by a smile and handshake---but only by massive violence and bloodshed.

The disagreeable issue was the despicable crime involving slavery of intelligent beings; which motivated the Empire to launch a "Correction."

This Correction was initiated by the Empire against a powerful System Lord known as the Ruler of Chud.

The Ruler of e Planet Chud was a huge creature. He was indescribably ugly and equally wicked.

Planet Chud was predominately a massive nursery for the Symbiotic offspring of the Ruler. This creature laid thousands of live Symbios per year; and so he needed cheap and intelligent help to care for them, until suitable hosts were found.

Occasionally the Ruler forced life forms into forced labor and implanted his Symbios into them---which was also against the law.

A TURN OF EVENTS

Anami and Kore Kordova were the strong sons of the System Lord, Sri and Dawn Kordova. They were the most respected family on P-8, Planet Centillion.

Planet Centillion was the govern-mental seat of the Centaurus Empire. Kore was the oldest of twin sons and expected to rule in the event of their father's death.

During the Police Action, Anami and Kore occupied the positions of Special Unit Commanders.

The two, identical twins were 6-2 and 225 pounds of ripped muscles. They looked like professional athletics; they were articulate, handsome and brilliant military strategists. The Empire was extremely proud of them.

During the Correction, they did irreparable damage to the war machine of the Ruler and his underlings, the Mutant Grays and the Throxs. They led the Empire troops in death-defying raids: Destroyed military bases, factories, fuel and supply depots; they severed the enemy's ability to advance or resupply, and thus the head of the serpent was cut off, and its body was slowly dying...

1980 Columbus, Ohio: Christina Santiago was eighteen years old, vibrant, a little headstrong but a good person. She was well-liked by her friends and even the teachers. She was a Freshman at Ohio State University in Columbus, Ohio.

Christina was driving her mother's black BMW. She picked up Liliana, her mother from work.

Liliana was a beautiful Hispanic lady of 40. She had long flowing black hair and a thick body.

> "You're here early", "Liliana said, with a warm smile. "but were you speeding again?
> "No, Mom, there wasn't any traffic near the Campus.
> "I want you to drive safely."

> "I do. I'm eighteen, and can handle anything life brings."
> "Okay invincible. I was like you at your age--- fearless." No one scared me. The word Fear was not in my vocabulary"
> "I won't bow to fear."

As Christina drove down an isolated country road. The summer air around them became electrically charged. Suddenly they're transported from the BMW into an orbiting spacecraft.

Moments later, they were in a white room. It looked like an operating room with sterile shiny stainless steel tables that were ice cold; and metal instruments placed neatly in metal trays.

Hanging from a nearby rack were several instruments that appeared to be flesh cutting saws and sharp curvy autopsy tools. Christina was on a Mu Galaxy-Class Cruiser, a Mutant Gray slave ship.

The Mutant Grays were alien beings; they were 4 ft tall, gray-colored, large heads, large almond-shaped eyes; they had no mouths but were expert ventriloquists.

The Mutant Gray vessel left orbit and headed out into

open space. The warp engines activated and they traveled at ten times the speed of light.

> "You're the last to fill the order," Dr. Q, the
> leader of the Mutant Grays tells her.
> "What order?"
> "Fortunate for you it's not human organs and
> body parts---at least not this time"

Christina looked to the left and saw Liliana. Christina tried to speak but no sound came from her mouth.
She tried repeatedly to get off the table, but failed because
of the metal restraint bands around her neck, torso, legs
and arms.   Their eyes met; Christina moved her lips
and formed the words: "I will not fear."

Liliana repeated the words in the same manner.
Christina was given an injection. She was unconscious.
Hours later, Christina awakened in a large room with
hundreds of teens and children. The children were
dressed in white jumpsuits. They also wore sandals.

Everyone in the room slept on thin mats. The light was
dim, the drone of the warp engines was a constant
background noise.

> "What is this place?" Christina asked.
> "No one knows," Lori Dawson, a ten year old
> answered. "I was on my way with my mother to
> the video store in Toledo, when two gray
> "things" grabbed both of us and brought us here.
> Most of the others had similar experiences. I'm so
> scared!" Lori cried.
> "Don't cry, Lori; somehow, things are going to
> work out. Where do they keep the grownups?"

"No one has seen their parents since arriving here. Whenever we ask the creatures about them, they pretend they don't understand. The last time I saw my mother was in that hospital-like room. I hope she's Okay. What's going to happen to us?

"I don't know what to make of all this. I've always heard that alien beings visited Earth on a regular basis; but the Government always denied the sightings. Now there's no doubt in my mind that aliens exist."

"Where do you think they're from?"

"No idea. But repeat this: "I will not fear," Christina said.

"What does that mean?"

"What I said: I will not fear," she repeated.

The children, many still in shock, repeated Christina's phrase until it became a mantra, a chant.

The Mutant Grays, who had hidden cameras and listening devices in the room, couldn't understand why the children were repeating the same words.

The Mutants failed to comprehend the emotional bond between the children--that they were not only miniature human beings but a glimpse of the entire Human Race; they were important individuals and part of the collective Race; they were loved by thousands who searched the Earth to find them; their disappearance broke many hearts, and stretched the faith of the faithful.

Several times a day, the door opened and children were taken to be examined by Dr. Q and his staff; all the children came back unharmed but visibly frightened.

Weeks went by. Then two Mutant Grays came for Christina and Lori. They were especially forceful, as though what awaited them was not an examination this time. The girls feared for their lives.

"You two are troublemakers; I have another pl- to put you," a Mutant told them. "And you're not going to like it. I told you several times to stop inciting the others, but you wouldn't listen. Now come with me!

Christina punched one of the Mutants in the face; she kicked the other one in the kneecap. Her kick-boxing course had paid off. But before she could strike again, the Mutants withdrew their weapons.

An explosion went off in the adjacent corridor. The Mutants holstered their weapons and left the children's room.

The alarm sounded: "Intruder Alert!" In the dim light, Centaurus Empire Soldiers mat- erialized in the corridor of the Mutant Gray ship. The soldiers threw Flash Grenades and Smoke Grenades into several rooms and rolled them down corridors. Other explosions rocked the ship and phaser weapons discharged. The Throxs were disoriented, recovered and retaliated in defense of the ship.

The Throxs, a reptile species, were the security force on the ship. They fought courageous and violently, but the element of surprise, level of training and marks- manship was on the side of the Empire.

Down the corridor raced eight heavily armed soldiers.

Mission Specialists Anami and Kore Kordova of the Centaurus Security Unit led the charge.

Their assignment was to capture or kill Dr. Q and his horde of humanoid traffickers; and the Throxs were completely irrelevant—shoot them on sight.

Kore Kordova took two other soldiers to find Dr. Q and investigate other parts of the ship. The ship was Massive, with many rooms and levels. The notorious Dr. Q could have been anywhere or even not on the ship.

Anami Kordova came into the room where Christina, Lori and the others were; the children were frightened and huddled in the corners.

> "I'm Anami Kordova of the Centaurus Empire Special Unit."
> "I'm Christina Santiago from the Planet Earth."
> "I've never heard of it, a planet called Earth. But we'll figure that out later. Right now, we have to secure this ship."

Meanwhile, Mission Specialist Kore and two soldiers entered the Laboratory. DR. Q and other Mutant Grays were in the room. Dr. Q had his back to Kore.

> "The elusive Dr. Q," Kore said with a sense of satisfaction. "I'm going to get a medal for this. You're going away for a long time"

Capturing or eliminating Dr. Q. would be a major achievement, an important step towards ending the three-year-old Correction.

Kore had become weary with the long hours spent tracking these criminals He looked forward to plenty of rest and relaxation on the Home World, Centillion.

Dr. Q turned around. He held a serpent-looking Symbios in his hand. Dr. Q threw the creature on Kore's neck. Kore struggled to knock it off, but the Symbios scrambles into his ear, bored a hole and entered his brain. Kore's eyes immediately flashed red: The Symbios gained access to Kore's mind.

> "This curse is from the Ruler of Chud: Kordova, you'll do evil deeds for the rest of your life; and you will serve my Symbios until you cut your own throat!"

Dr. Q and his crew were tried, convicted and sentenced to Life without any possibility of being free again. They were confined in a Maximum Security Facility on an orbiting moon.

Since Planet Earth wasn't on the Centaurus Star Charts, the children on the Mutant Gray slave ship were transported to Planet Centillion; and since the two species were genetically compatible, the Humans were accepted and integrated into the general population.

The adults weren't on the ship, and were believed to had been transported off the ship---either back to Earth or onto another vessel, where they would be sold as slaves, food or replacement parts.

A week later, the Correction came to an end.
After being compromised by the evil Symbios, Kore

Kordova was committed to a mental hospital for observation and removal of the Symbios.

SRI KORDOVA DIES

Anami Kordoba and Christine Santiago soon became close friends. Then one day Anami asked her to become his wife. There was a great wedding with dignitaries from over three hundred planets.

Sri Kordova, though 200 years old and frail, was present and had a good time. But three days later, while in bed and on their Honeymoon, Anami received an urgent message.

"Christina, It's my father. The doctors say that he won't make it through the night. I have to go to him."

"I'll get dressed and go with you. If this is his last day, I want to be with you and him."

They arrived at his bedside. Anami took his father's hand; Christina stood nearby. Sri Kordova spoke:

"Thank you for coming at this late hour. I know you're on your Honeymoon, but I've put off dying as long as I could."

"Sure you don't want to stick around another hundred years?"

"No my son, it's time for you to reign. Anami Kordova, I charge you with the great responsebility to rule the Empire with wisdom and a mighty hand. My friends are now your friends; my enemies are your enemies.

Second: I want you to find my son Kore and bring him back home; do all that you can to spare his life; but don't lose yours in the process.

And lastly: The Ruler of Chud must die; he's been a thorn in my side for 80 years; he corrupted Kore just to torment me; he'll continue to be the same to you. How you dispose of him is up to you. Do these things and I'll rest in peace."
"I will do as you have said."
"Christina, I charge you to take care of Anami. You're the best thing that ever happened to him. Love him and stand by him--- just like Dawn, his mother loved me for 142 years before she passed on to the higher plane."
"I'll always love him," Christina assured him, "with all my heart, body and soul."

Sri Kordova nodded, then he died. The beloved Leader was given a grandiose sending off. System Lords and Planetary Officials filed by his open casket; loyal subjects wept and others held back their tears; even his enemies showed up---to make sure that he was dead!

But his arch enemy, the System Lord known as the Ruler of Chud, was not present, neither did he send a representative or even a message of condolence.

FREE AT LAST

Kore Kordova was confined to a Mental Ward design-ed to treat infectious diseases and parasites; the Symbios was considered a parasite, although several cultures will-fully merge with them to produce longer life and resilie-nce in harsh atmospheres and terrain.

Though he was the brother to the reigning System Lord afforded him creature comfort and respect, but he wasn't allowed to leave.

Kore walked into the Doctor's Office. He was accompanied by his attendant, Nurse Faye Furtura.

Faye Furtura---Fabulous Faye, as she was called--- was slender with voluptuous breasts, apple-bottom butt and secretary legs. She had long blond hair and green eyes. Her nurse uniform looked to be ready to explode. She was classy, and several doctors had proposed marriage to her, but she turned them down.

"Your test look promising," Dr. Fair told Kore. "I see no reason why we can't do the brain surgery tomorrow Morning."

"Tomorrow Morning? Uh---but you said it's exploratory to see if the Symbios can be removed. What if it would rather kill me than be removed?"

"It's true this is the first attempt to remove an unwanted Symbios from the Ruler's Spawn; but we've had success with other types of Symbios."

"I'm told there's none like the one I have. I'm in control until I get stressed-out."

"Kore, how do you really know--- when you think you're in control, it's in control then too? This Symbios may be deceptive beyond your senses. We have a 95% chance of removing it."

"Five percent is a small risk. Let's do this."

Kore and Nurse Faye left the Doctor's Office. They arrived at his private suite within the hospital.

As soon as they closed the door, Faye pushed him against the wall and they kissed passionately."I'm so hot!" Faye told him. "I wanted to rip your clothes off in the Doctor's Office!"

"Do you think they know about us?" Kore asked her. They had been sleeping together for three months.

"Do "Do you think they even care? You're a war hero, a highly decorated soldier, and the brother of the System Lord."

"You know I should have been the next System Lord. I'm the elder brother."

"I know honey. I've got the password to the Main Entrance and everyone is in place," she said very excited.

"You're a good woman Faye, and I promise to marry you as soon as I'm out of here."

"You've better lay claim to all this!" She wiggles her butt with hands on hips.

They held hands and went into the bedroom. They undressed and made love on top of the covers.

That night, when Faye's shift was over, they left the Mental Hospital. Kore keep his promise. On his way to a private craft, he stopped at a Marriage Clerk and married Faye.

CHAPTER TWO
A TIME TO HEAL

Five years passed since the Correction against the Ruler of Chud and Mutant Grays, and the death of Sri Kordova.

The reigning System Lord, Anami Kordova, was charged with the awesome task of securing and re-building the Empire including the economy; it costs the Empire tremendous resources to halt the expansion and illegal activities of the Ruler.

He and Christina hadn't the luxury of a long Honeymoon before he was thrust into ruling the entire Centaurus Empire. Fortunate for Anami that his father had several trusted Officials to assist him.

Planet Centillion, the Home World of the Centaurus Empire, was an Earth-like planet, yet with only one large continent surrounded by deep blue ocean.

Hundreds of cargo freighters emerged from deep space. They paused and became visible for only a moment, transported their cargos to the surface and quickly departed. Passenger and civilian crafts also shared the expanse of space.

Though business was booming for the Empire, it was al-also ripe pickings for the bandits, pirates, renegades and disgruntle individuals, sore losers from the Correction, and some were terrorists for various ideological reasons.

After the Correction and the incarceration of high level criminals, a vacuum emerged, and a new breed of criminals; it seemed like overnight, a crime wave swept the galaxy; space piracy, the hijacking of merchant ships, cargo freighters and space trains became a major concern for the Galactic Security Force.

It was reported that the pirates had fast and heavily armored ships, the latest of stolen technology and weapons; all in all, they made the Galactic Security Force tremble whenever they came upon these fortified ships.

It soon became common knowledge that the Empire was plagued by organized criminals called the League. The mastermind of this band of outlaws was Kore Kordova, also known as Alien Kore because of the evil Symbios living in his brain.

Led by the Symbios, shortly after Kore escaped from the Mental Hospital, he rendezvoused with hundreds of outlaws and agents of the Ruler and because the leader of the League.

What Sri Kordova warned Anami about the menace and continued threat the Ruler posed to the Empire was becoming more apparent every day.

But the Empire struck back: On Planet P-7734 a secret weapon was completed. P-7734 was an industrial planet; it had binary red suns and was therefore very hot. Only those who lived there were used to the searing heat.

The binary suns hung near like to bloodshot eyes; one to the East and the other to the West. In the Evening, the eyes crossed but never went completely down.

P-7734 was a wealth of metals and mineral deposits. The mines produced megatons of base and rare metals used in the manufacturing of spacecraft hulls and their internal components.

Warp Drive Crystals, plasma injectors, warp cores, and heat-resistant computer chips were also manufactured and assembled on this world, making it extremely valuable to the Empire.

The System Lord: Anami Kordova, Commander Hur, Greman Outto and ten Empire Officials inspected the new Weapon System.

Commander Hur, was in his mid 50s; he was medium height, stout, square shouldered, had a granite jaw, with a fatherly look on his face. He also had a deep authoritarian voice that commanded respect. Hur was a trusted Official and close friend of Sri Kordova, and now worked beside Anami Kordova.

Greman Outto was an obese man. At 5-5 and six hundred pounds. He was always sweaty, and made friction sounds when he walked.

Though Greman Outto was a sight to see, he was also a genius and the chief Defense Contractor for the Empire.

"The VXT Interceptor is your answer to utterly crush the League," Greman told them in a matter-of-fact tone.
"Its onboard crystal-powered computers can track 250 targets at a distance of 5 light years; its improved titanium-crushed diamond hull, and

pulse-alternating shields can deflect every weapon know to us; its stealth ability is 100% with modest power consumption; its four concealed Plasma-Crystal Warp Drive II Engines can cruise at Warp 8, with maximum velocity of Warp 10.5.

Its weapon package are 1,000 programmable proton mini-missiles and six Red Plasma Gatling Guns. I have saved the best for last: The VXT can open a stable worm hole while in the atmosphere of any planet; this will come in handy in emergency departure."

"Take a breath Greman," Anami Kordova interjected, "we're al-ready sold on it. Greman, "I'm ready to take possession of this prototype as soon as possible."

The shimmering black VXT flew by overhead at a high rate of speed. It went through several maneuvers before it returned and hovered above them.

"We'll pick it up tomorrow Morning; I will expect another thousand by the end of the year."
"You've made an excellent decision," Outto said.

Outto wiped the sweat from his fat face with what looked like a bed sheet.

"It's always a pleasure doing business with the Empire. I'll personally guarantee quality workmanship and prompt delivery. The prototype will be coded for transport."
"Good work. I knew I could depend on you.. Now let me get out of here before I pass out from the heat," Anami told him.

TO STEAL A MOCKINGBIRD

Kore Kordova, known mainly as Kore, sat in the Captain's Chair of his ship, the Heavy Metal. The ship was cloaked above Planet 7734.

His Navigator, Scarface was with him. Scarface was a creature with four arms and looked like a cross between an octopus and Human. His face was scared from knife wounds and pitted from shrapnel and blunt force traumas.

> "You've really outdone yourself Scarface; It's beautiful how you redesigned and refitted this Cargo Freighter into a formable war machine."
> "Anything for you Kore."
> "Contact Boris Monday. Tell him were out of time."
> "I've transmitted the Code to Monday. It's ready; I've locked onto the Weapon with the transporter Beam. Energized."

Kore stole the VXT Interceptor from its hanger. It was transported to the Cargo Bay aboard the Heavy Metal. Kore activated a device on his belt, and transported himself and Scarface from the Bridge to the Cargo Bay. As they materialized in the Cargo Bay, they saw Boris Monday, his help in stealing the Interceptor.

Boris Monday was a handsome and resourceful person. He was 6 feet tall, 185 pounds, and in his early forties. He liked wearing expensive clothes and jewelry. So to finance his flamboyant lifestyle, he robbed for Greman and gave to the Kore.

"We have the VXT!" Kore exclaimed and grinned.

"But the blueprints for the VXT weren't in Gremen's safe. We'll have to reverse engineer to duplicate it."

PRISON BREAK

Moments later, the Heavy Metal dropped out of warp near a moon orbiting Centaurus; it was the Centaurus Maximum Security Facility. The facility housed 1500 dangerous criminals. Many were captured during the Correction and sentenced to rot on this desolate moon.

The prison was heavily guarded and monitored electronically. No space-craft was to pass within 100 miles of the moon without Empire escort.

A squadron of Interceptors sat on the runway to discourage the daring and curious. Several anti-spacecraft guns were mounted and aimed at the sky. Razor wire draped the top of the 30-ft. walls.

Outside the prison warning signs were posted: "Beware of Giant Scorpions!" The scorpions lived in the cold lunar sands that surrounded the prison. The giant scorpions were visible and aggressive during the day. They pounded their tails against the stone walls, in an attempt to get to the occupants of the prison.

The VXT left the Cargo Bay of the Heavy Metal. It materialized above the prison walls.

Kore's eyes glowed as the Symbios took control.
Kore fired two proton mini-missiles: The prison defenses, anti-spacecraft platforms and Control Center were destroyed with a brilliant flash. Kore fired the rotating white plasma Gatling Guns. They vaporized the

guard towers and everyone in them. Kore blasted a large hole in the outer wall. In seconds, the giant Scorpions came into the prison.

The guards were immediately engaged in a death match with the giant scorpions. The scorpions they could kill, but the VXT with its advanced shielding remained untouched and a persistent threat.

The scorpions whipped their agile poisonous, sharp tails and impelled the guards, often lifting them off their feet high into the air; then they snapped their tails like a whip, and the guards sailed through the air and smashed against the walls and buildings.

The prisoners, being on 24 hour lockdown and living deep within the prison, were in an underground vault.

Meanwhile, Scarface locked onto and transported the prisoners to the Cargo Hold of the Heavy Metal.

As the VXT reached escape velocity, Kore fired two Incinerator Missiles from the aft launchers. The missiles vaporized the remainder of the prison.

Kore, Scarface and DR. Q, a Mutant Gray Scientist stood on the Bridge. The attack on the prison was to free Dr. Q and 1500 people loyal to the Ruler and to Kore; and some were just criminals with their own agendas.

"Welcome back Dr. Q." Kore greeted in a flat tone.

He didn't like or trust Dr. Q. The Doctor was responsible for the misery in Kore's life. But the Ruler and the

Symbios had an agreement, and working arrangement with Dr. Q, and Kore was powerless to do anything about that; he also needed Doctor Q for this mission.

"Good to be alive and among the living."
"That could change if you don't give me the coordinates to Earth."

Dr. Q went to the Navigation Console and entered coordinates into the computer.

"That should do it," Dr. Q began. "For years I've keep the location to Earth from the Empire and the other System Lords."
"A lot of good the secret would do you in prison; now all of us have someplace to go far away from the Empire. If what you told me about the people of Earth is true, I'll set myself up as their System Lord in no time at all."

The ship sped along at high warp for a few minutes, and intercepted a Military Space Train.

Again, the Heavy Metal dropped out of warp, but remained cloaked. General Urich transported onto the Bridge. General Urich was Kore's Second-in Command. He also operated the Weapons Console. The General was 6-8, brawny build, bald, mean-looking and never smiled. He always wore a full-length black leather coat with matching pants and boots. Gen. Urich was never actually a General, but Kore gave him the title.

The Military Space Train, heavily armored with twenty boxcars came within missile range. It had two massive locomotives attached. The military escorts were two Empire Interceptors.

The Heavy Metal materialized on the Port Side of the Interceptors.

"Destroy the escorts," Kore ordered.

In their sneak attack, General Urich at the Weapon's Console, fired two proton missiles and destroyed the escorts.

"Open hailing frequency," Kore told Scarface.
"Engineer Parks, resistance is futile: Stand down and prepare to be boarded."

Engineer Parks was 100 years old. He was 5-8 and weighs 125 pounds. His hair was gray. He dressed like a traditional Earth Railroad Engineer.

"I've been on this line for 50 years and haven't lost a train," Parks firmly stated, "and I'm not about to lose this one!"
"Old fellow, as sure as you now have breath, I'll take your train and your life."
"There was once a time when I knew you as the honorable son of the greatest System Lord that ever lived."
"Stand down and prepare to be boarded!"

Kore's eyes glowed and he spoke in a deep alien voice. Parks thought it best to give up the train. Then Kore, Gen. Urich and another Elite Guardsmen transported onto the Bridge of the Space Train.

The Bridge of the locomotive was computerized, neat and clean. The Bridge crew of the Space Train consisted of four humanoids, young Cadets in their twenties, and six Android AIs.

Parks tried to hold back his anger but failed. He knew Kore when Kore was a baby, and couldn't believe that he had fallen so low in morality.

"You're a despicable disgrace!" Parks blurted.

Again Kore's eyes glowed blood red: Again the Symbios spoke in a deep and harsh voice.

"There's no fool like an old fool. You will not talk to Me that way. Eject him!"

General Urich took a black hood from his pocket. He slipped the hood over Park's head. Parks was marched to a nearby airlock. Parks was placed inside the airlock; the outer door opened and Parks was jettisoned into outer space.

"Anyone else have a problem with me?"

The Cadets were scared and horrified; one Cadet urinated on himself. They shook their heads for "no."

Kore, Gen. Urich and Scarface inspected the hijacked train. In the cars were captured Mu Galaxy-Class Cruiser (Mutant Gray technology) parts, weapon systems, small arms, missiles, warheads, explosives, electronic components, and a Stargate. Most of this was in transit to be scrapped or destroyed.

The AIs were deactivated and taken. The Cadets were placed in a disabled shuttle and left behind.

After getting on the way, Kore entered his quarters;

it was a plain Freighter Captain's Quarters found on any merchant ship---except a King Size bed was added.

Faye greeted him at the door. This time, without her nurse's uniform. Faye looked and dressed like a Supermodel. She wore tight clothes that revealed her figure. She talked and walked seductively.

"I hope you're not walking around the ship dressed like this," Kore said with a smile.

"No, I'm looking like this just for your eyes only. How was your day?"

"It's not like I have a real job; but I get things done. Every day is a new adventure."

"You're a fearless leader. I love a male who sees what he wants and goes after it."

"Thanks, I'm good at going after things---people too. Look, this journey will be long, and I have a ship full of violent people; so be careful when outside the quarters. One of these fools might try to murder me on account of you."

"We won't let that happen, will we? Anyway, I Hope the Human females are fashion conscious. I need a new wardrobe. I heard there are Malls and other places to buy clothes, shoes and everything a female needs."

"The Human females are called Women; and they shop until they drop. We have a few living on Centillion that were rescued years ago from a Mutant Gray slave ship. Have you talked to any of them?"

"No, I only saw them on the Evening News. But I do know that Empress Christina is a Human."

"That's right. Anami bagged him a good one."

"And I've bagged you!"

Faye kissed Kore. She dimmed the lights. Faye lead Kore to the bed by his utility belt, then dropped it on the floor. She undressed Kore down to his underwear, pushed him back on the bed, climbed on top, straddled him, and passionately kissed him. They made love.

THE RIPPER

As they journeyed to Earth, Kore rendezvoused with groups loyal to his cause. They were the usual lot found in every civilization; some were terrorists. The majority of them were wanted for serious crimes against the Empire.

They were mercenaries, assassins, bounty hunters, military deserters, escapees, space pirates, smugglers, drug dealers, prostitutes, and those whose ideologies or lifestyles were frowned upon by society; they were the misfits of the universe.

Still others actually held positions in commerce and governments; they were medical doctors, lawyers, scientists, professors and technical personnel, who had lost their way and found themselves following Kore.

With those he already had aboard, his crew numbered two thousand. Kore had thousands of followers. But for this assignment, he chose those whose physical appearance wouldn't stand out in the world he was going to conquer.

But the Mutant Grays and Scarface were the exceptions. He needed their brains, not their looks. He planned to keep them from public view.

However during the long journey, someone aboard was a predator. They roamed the corridors at night, stalked and butchered crewmembers.

Kore assigned General Urich to investigate and jettison the killer off the ship; but the General couldn't catch the culprit, though he laid several traps.

One night, the killer waited in the closet of a female crewmember. She entered her quarters. The killer leaped out the closet and plunged a machete-type knife into her chest, pulled it out, then cut her throat. The crewmember crumpled to the floor; she choked in her own blood. This was the fifth such killing.

In the Morning after the last murder: Kore called the General into a private room.

> "General, this is the fifth murder committed on this ship. Do you have any idea who it is?"
> "I'm still working on it."
> "If they keep killing the crew, we won't have anyone left when we reach Earth. In fact, they might wind up killing me and Faye."
> "I won't let that happen. I'll double the guard around your quarters."
> "I don't need panic among the crew; they're already dangerous; no need to make them paranoid too."

The warp engines trudged through space carrying the outlaws and their stolen space train loaded with war materials.

Life on the freighter was barbaric. Tempers flared; the desire to resolve conflicts with fist and weapons was in their mental makeup. Kore confiscated the most dangerous weapons and locked them away.

They drank and fought over the prostitutes and those females who weren't for sale. The ones the serial killer didn't get---which now amounted to twelve--lost their lives or were injured in drunken fights.

At least once a week the dead were jettisoned from the ship; no service held or words spoken over them; they were jettisoned with the daily garbage, and few even cared.

The Mutant Grays were passive aggressive beings. They spent most of the time on the computers and in their laboratory; they brainstormed and constructed electronic devices from the available resources. They reprogrammed the Androids to follow Kore's orders. The Grays also activated and reprogrammed the Artificial Intelligence Units(AI) that were stored, plus reassembled weapon systems and warp drive engines from the Military Space Train.

Kore protected the Mutant Grays from the rest of the crew. He threatened to throw anyone into space if they harmed his scientists. Kore needed beings who could think, and not just pull a trigger.

After a year in space they arrived at Earth.

The vessels were cloaked. Kore parked the convoy on the far side of Earth's Moon. Out of Human view, Kore made the Moon his initial base of operation.

"There's a lot of criminal activity on this planet," Scarface observed as he monitored the communication satellites orbiting Earth. They even have terrorists organizations."

"Our research showed that those who appear Human to them will easily assimilate into this civilization," Dr. Q told them. "There's a broad diversity of races and cultures."

"So unless they catch us trans-porting about, they won't suspect a thing," Monday added.

"Humans, meet your System Lord!"

"Hope you're not planning to broadcast that ominous message!" Dr. Q added.

"No, that won't work; they're not primitive, or can be persuaded that we're their god or something; no, first we have to weaken them--- bring them to their knees."

Scarface seemed confused.

"Why Earth?"

"Earth has natural resources; the other planets are also rich in metals. I'll build an armada of ships this area of the Milky Way has ever seen."

CHAPTER THREE
HEAVY IS THE HEAD

In space near Planet Centillion, twelve warships parked outside of orbit.

Below, Anami Kordova called an emergency meeting with the Synod of System Lords. The System Lords were of different species. They were dressed in their respective royal attire.

All of them were at Sri Kordova's funeral: The System Lords at this meeting were: Emperor Vox, Lord Premosee, and Queen Wench-Desiree.

Emperor Vox was green and ten foot tall, Lord Premosee was large, weighed 1200 pounds. He was Cobra-looking. Queen Wench-Desiree was a humanoid female who was and looked a decrepit 2000 years old.

The room was large with an oval--shaped conference table. Anami stood at the end of the conference table.

"I assure you," Anami began, "Kore will be brought to justice for every act of lawlessness the League he and the League committed in our territories."

"Heavy is the head that wears the crown, Emperor Vox began, "In the past," we've placed utmost confidence in the wisdom and direction of Sri Kordova to lead the Synod; now, if you want the same respect and consideration, this Alien Kore lawlessness must come to an end!"

"We sympathize that it's your brother," Lord Premosee added," but it seems the alien Symbios has overpowered him, and it's not Kore Kordova we're dealing with, but the alien Symbios."

"I believe that Kore is still in there, and can be rescued," Anami countered.

"If you don't apprehend Alien Kore, we'll kill him ourselves!" Queen Wench-Desiree snapped.

"Come now, Wench," Lord Premosee interjected, "don't talk that way; this is a delicate situation; if we can't stand united with this new System Lord and this great Empire—then what are we doing here?"

"Thank you Lord Premosee, Anami added, "I know the Synod is results-oriented; I promise not to disappoint you."

The Synod immediately transported back to their warships. One by one they achieved warp velocity and disappeared in the dark heavens.

EMPRESS KORDOVA

Christina Santiago, now Empress Christina, Comdr. Hur and Lt. Dawson entered the room. Christina was 5-7, athletic build, silky skin and Hispanic. She usually had a positive, cheerful disposition.

Lt. Dawson, a young petite woman, was professional in her work and behavior. She had red hair and "ginger" complexion. The two first met on the Mutant Gray slave ship. She had come a long way from the scared and freckled child. She was educated in the best schools, graduated top in her class, and went on to become a respected Officer .

"Good news," Comdr. Hur greeted." Capt. Granger of the Starship Thor reported he picked up the ionized particle trail and warp signature of the stolen Military Space Train. The train was on course to the destination marked on the star chart as "unexplored.""

"We questioned Dr. Q's colleagues and personal enemies on his home world, " Lt. Dawson added, "and confiscated Dr. Qs notes and charts. I recognize one chart as being where Earth is located."

"Yes, I too recognize the star formations," Christina added, "we call them the Zodiac Signs. Earth is the third of nine planets orbiting a star!

Comdr. Hull laughed. They make it sound so easy.

"We'll know which star when we get closer. But the warp drive on the Space Train needed minor repairs. Kore probably unaware of it, but he left a trail of bread crumbs through space."

"Excellent work!"

"Three Starships are fueled and ready," Comdr. Hur assured him.

Later that day, the Kordovas were having a quiet dinner together. Usually they dined with family, friends, or government officials. But tonight was special.

Somehow, they avoided talking about Earth after leaving the Council Chambers. But the pink elephant was in the room, and no one wanted to talk about it. A long table separated them.

"Husband, will you allow me to visit Earth?" She broke the silence.

He acted surprised.

"Why Empress Christina, I'm shocked that you would even ask such a thing. There's no one else I would have accompany me on a 17,000 light year journey. I wouldn't love you enough if I withheld such joy from you."

She ran to his end of the table, sat on his lap and kissed him passionately on the lips.

"Christina, I love you. I have never loved anyone more than you. Your presence brightens up my life and this whole kingdom. The citizens love you too."
"That's sweet of you to say that. I was concerned you'd think I wouldn't come back. I didn't marry you because I thought I'd never go home again; I married you because I love you. And if I found you on Earth, I would still have married you!"
"You know me, I often think too much."
"Then think about changing the length of this table, so I can sit beside you."
"When we get back from Earth, I'll decree that Empress Christina can sit beside her husband at dinner!"
"I'm surprised we're allowed to sleep in the same bed," she joked. "Some changes need to be made around here."
"I've been saying that for years; it's been the old ways in new times; my father liked things the way they've been for the last hundred years."

"Getting back to the subject, can Lori and I tell the others that we've found Earth?"

"Yes, tell them they can relocate to Earth---or even visit for a while."

"It's a tough decision," Christina reasoned, "because many of them are married and have children. It would be terrible if these families split up."

"Let's hope that doesn't happen; I believe in the family structure. And if the citizens of Earth are friendly and willing to talk, great possibilities exist."

"Is there anything else, dear?"

"Yes, find Lt. Dawson and get to work."

THE CAVERN

Cloaked invisibly, Kore brought the Heavy Metal into Earth orbit. Kore sat in the Captain's chair. He monitored news reports and surfed the Internet.

Scarface and others are at their stations. Boris Monday came on the Bridge.

"My Intelligence Team is ready," Monday reported to Kore. "Each of my operatives has been issued documents and currency.

"Your mission is, by any means necessary, get control of and subdue these Humans."

Scarface became agitated, overly excited by what he saw on the ship's sensor array.

"I've found the perfect ground base. It's in the Hindu Kush Mountains, in a country called Afghanistan."

"What is it?"

"A natural cavern with no surface entrance. It's over a mile beneath the surface."

"Sounds like my kind of place. Let's go."

Kore, Gen. Urich, Scarface, Monday and four Elite Guards equipped with respirator masks, transported into the Cavern. All were dressed in body armor and armed.

The Cavern was spacious and dark. They turned on portable lamps to see. Jagged rocks protruded from the ceiling, walls and floor.

"This is exactly what we need. Get the engineers down here and let's make this our new home."

AFGHANISTAN

Afghanistan was a rugged country. Over half of it consisted of high plateaus and mountain ranges such as the Hindu Kush Mountains. The country was landlocked and approx. 251, 800 square miles, slightly smaller than Texas. Iran was to the West, Pakistan to the South-East. Afghanistan had 27 million people.

In 1979 the Soviet Union invaded Afghanistan to support their pro-Soviet Government. This led to the formation of an opposition group called the Mujahideen (Islamic Warriors), and other local tribal chiefs called warlords.

The Taliban took power in 1990; the Mujahideen received international help when evidence was presented that the Taliban supported Saudi-born terrorist Osama Bin Laden and his Al-Queda terrorists network.

Terrorists attacks became frequent throughout the world: Embassies, military bases, ships, hotels, trains, schools and roadside checkpoints were bombed. But when the terrorists attacked America, the mighty war machine of the United States arrived in Afghanistan.

CHAPTER FOUR
THE EARTH MARSHALL

Dressed in Afghan garments, Kore and several Elites materialized in a cave; they remained out of sight. There were thirty Mujahideen warriors in the cave.

The leader of the terrorists was Sanballat Hadad, a ruthless warlord. Sanballat Hadad was a lanky, bearded man about 5-10 in height. He was dressed in a robe, sandals, and had a white turban on his head.

Kore and his troops silently materialized behind them. At the sound of Kore's voice, they turned to grab their AK-47 assault rifles, but stopped short of touching them; Kore and his soldiers had weapons trained.

> "We come in peace. We're on the same side, "Kore announced.
> "Sounds like what the KGB and CIA told us several years ago," Sanballat replied dryly. "I'm Sanballat Hadad, leader of the Mujahideen.
> "I'm known as Alien Kore."
> "What an odd name," Sanballat countered.
> "You will understand later. But now, I have a proposition for you.
> "Have your soldiers lower their weapons and we can talk. By the way, what type of weapons are those?"

Kore ignored the request and the question.

"I represent the League, an association of opportunists

willing to finance your struggle. The infidels have taken over your country and stolen your crude oil. Let us help you. We'll supply you with finances, state-of-the-art weapons and complete systems that will enable you to drive the Coalition Forces from the entire Middle East, or wipe them from the face of the Earth."

Sanballat and his warriors laughed in Kore's face. They thought Kore was insane, on drugs or delirious from drinking sea water.

"You must take me for a fool!"

Kore paused, then pressed a button on his utility belt. Kore transported himself, Sanballat, and the landing party to the Bridge of the Heavy Metal.

The Heavy Metal was in a fixed orbit above the Arabian Sea. On the large view screen was Afghanistan, Iran, Pakistan and other countries. At a short distance, the International Space Station was seen.

"We're visitors to your world looking to make it our home.

Kore reaches in his pocket and withdraws a velvet pouch full of cut diamonds. He hands it to Sanballat. Sanballat dumped the diamonds into his hand. He nodded affirmatively.

"These are worth millions: What is it we can do for you?"
"It's not only what you can do for us, but what we can do for you. We're sympathetic to your cause---to the extent of pouring billions into it.

In return you'll represent my interest and become my Earth Marshal.

Scarface interrupted them:

"Kore, we have a problem."

Scarface put it on the views screen.   They observed a Special Forces Team accompanied by Afghan troops nearing the cave entrance where Sanballat's warriors were.

"General, take care of this."

The General, from the Weapons Console, fired several short micro bursts. He ambushed the Special Forces Team. The Team didn't know what hit them. Their energy-scorched bodies laid disfigured and contorted by the severe heat.

"That's only a sample of what we can do," Kore boasted.
"Alien Kore, we have a deal."

Sanballat was returned to his cave and warriors.

His men were amazed that he disappeared and reappeared. They thought it had religious significance.

"You wouldn't believe what my eyes have seen!" Sanballat exclaimed.

K-2 UZBEKISTAN

Uzbekistan was located north of Afghanistan. K-2 was a covert American base that used to belong to the Soviet Union, who were driven out of Afghanistan. Now the base was used by the United States 5th Special Forces Group---America's stone-cold killers; and the CIA---America's conflict starters.

From K-2, the Green Berets killed 31,000 enemy combatants in Afghanistan alone. They were also responsible for training and arming the Northern Alliance against the Taliban and Al-Queda.

Lt. Col. John Mack, a husky rock-jawed soldier, was worried about his men. It was two hours past the check-in time. Mack was like a father to his men; some of them needed that relationship. He stood by the radio operator and waited. Finally, he made the call.

"Pit Bull, this is Lucky Strike, come in."

There was no reply. He called Bagnam Airfield North of Kabul, Afghanistan. They handled most of his airstrikes.

"Dark Wing, this is Lucky Strike: I lost my Pit Bulls along the Timur Pass; check on them."
"Will do, Lucky Strike."

The airfield diverted an Apache Helicopter to the area. Before they got there, the helicopter came under attack from a ZSU-23-4 Soviet Antiaircraft Gun, manned by Taliban fighters. The helicopter landed in a safe area.

"Dark Wing, this is Rolling Stones, we've got a ZSU!" The crew loaded the dead Berets and Afghans.

Moments later, a guided missile hit the antiaircraft gun.

When the chopper arrived at K-2, Col. Mack met them. When he saw the condition of his men, he winced.

"What happened to my boys? Take them to the infirmary. I want some answers and want them fast!"

THE MIDAS TOUCH

Time had passed and the Cavern renovation continued. Kore and Faye settled into their quarters. Faye decorated the room and made it a love nest. A huge canopy bed was in the middle of the room. It has fluffy pillows and stuffed animals on it. She even has a teacup poodle which she carried in her purse everywhere she went.

It was morning, and Kore finished making love to Faye. He got out of bed to get dressed.\; but Faye reaches out to stop him.

"Come back, I'm not satisfied yet. I'm still full of love. Don't you want some more?"
"Yes, but I've work to do. And while I'm gone, keep your hot ass away from the crew. I see the way they look at you when you walk around the Cavern. "
"There you go again; you're jealous!"
"Yeah, among my other issues--what else is new? Faye, You have an effect on males.
"I can't help the way males look at me---as long as they don't touch the merchandise"
"I trust you Faye, I just don't trust them. I can't stand a male whose servicing my female and claims that he's loyal to me."

"Anyway, if you love me so much why don't you take me outside the Cavern, because I'm dying to go shopping!?"

"Shopping is overrated."

"Kore, darling, I know you didn't mean that. I read that on Earth, not allowing a woman to shop is cruel and unusual punishment!"

She jokingly shook her little fist at him.

"When you were a baby--you must not have been breast-fed."

"That's it; no more satellite television for you. Leave my mother out of it. Now, I have to go and make some money.

"Are you serious?"

"No, watch all the television you want. Take care, I'll be home soon."

"Will you take me shopping afterwards?"

"Yeah, to Paris, France."

"You're lying!"

"It's what I do best."

"Maybe next to what you do best…"

When he arrived on the Bridge of the Heavy Metal, Gen. Urich and Boris Monday met him.

"Did you sleep well?" Boris asked.

"Like a grizzly bear in a short Winter. I felt that any moment the ceiling would come down and crush Faye and me. I've faced the fact that I'm not like the Human terrorists: I like comfort; and I would never strap on a bomb and blow myself up for any reason. "

"You promised Sanballat weapons," Scarface

Scarface reminded him, "But if we give Sanballat and his warriors our energy weapons they may kill us first, and then the Coalition Forces. We have a stockpile diamonds in our treasury."

"I could counterfeit a few million dollars," Boris added.

"No," Kore shook his head, "one thing I've learned about commerce, is to use other people's money."

The Heavy Metal established a fixed orbit over the United States. The view screen zoomed in on a large stone building near Fort Knox, Kentucky.

The building was the U.S. Gold Bullion Depository. It was used to store a large portion of the U.S. official gold reserves. It held 4,603 tons of gold bullion. It was second in the U.S. only to the Federal Reserve Bank of New York's underground vault in Manhattan, which held 5,000 tons of gold bullion. Below the building lay the gold vault, which was lined with granite walls and protected by a 22-ton blast-proof door. No single person was entrusted with the combination; beyond the door, the vault was protected by numerous layers of physical security, alarms, video cameras and sensors.

The fortress was surrounded by several fences and patrolled by armed guards of the U.S. Mint Police. The Depository was also protected by Fort Knox, a U.S. Army Base. On the base were Apache Helicopter gunships of the 4/229 Aviation, the 16th Cavalry Regiment, the Army Armor School, and the 3rd Brigade Combat Team; together totaling 30,000 soldiers with tanks and artillery.

"Energize," Kore ordered.

The transporter beam ripped through the atmosphere, penetrated the exterior of the Depository, and the probe-sensors locked on to entire pal-lets of .900-999 fine gold. Kore transported the gold via the ship to a room in the Cavern. The gold never materialized on the ship transporter plates.

This was Kore's scheme: The technicians in the Cavern would process the gold through their conversion machine; the conversion machine would change the appearance of the gold, it's size and weight to that of London Good Delivery bars of bullion that weighed 400 troy ounces each. The London gold bar was eight inches long, and stamped on top with a reputable manufacturer's name; the gold would become "commodity gold" and could be purchased by any private citizen or organization. In the end, the gold bars would look like they came from London or Zurich. Each London gold bar was worth $384,000. The estimated worth of Kore's gold heist was $137 Billion U.S. Dollars!

> "The Internet is a wonderful tool," Kore said, "an alien can learn all he needs to know to conquer this civilization while parked in space."

Alarms sounded in the Depository. The guards searched the video screens for the intruder. They checked the system panels for malfunctions. The automatic distress signal went to Fort Knox; soldiers were on the way. But there was no intruder; the floor sensors activated, because there was no longer any weight on the floors.

Capt. Fleming of the Mint Police rushed to the vault with his men: The entire depository of U.S. gold was gone. Even the steel pallets it sat on were gone.

"How can anyone steal a whole room of gold right under my nose," he said aloud to himself. "And why did this have to happen on my watch? There goes my job!"

Next on the agenda, Kore maneuvered the Heavy Metal and took a cloaked but fixed position over North Carolina. Fort Bragg came on the view screen. This was the home of the Special Forces, Green Berets. The target: The warehouse cache of special weapons, explosives and electronic devices used in covert operations throughout the world. The warehouse was complexed. It was arranged in such a manner that he had to hand-pick what he wanted.

"Lower the Transporter Ring", Kore ordered.

The Rings descended. Then he and a dozen Elites transported. The rings lifted and they were ambushed. Six Military Police opened up with automatic weapons fire. They sprayed the thieves with a hail of hot lead.

However, the bullets bounced off the Elite's body armor. The terrorists returned fire; the M.P.s weren't so lucky. Two of the M.P.s received direct chest hits and died; two others fail unconscious from their wounds; the other ran for help.

"Someone watch the door," Kore ordered. He was shaken by the surprise. "The rest start port-tagging those crates over there, there, there, and there," he quickly pointed.

Each soldier had an anti-gravitational wand that levitated the crates to the Transporter Rings.

Previously, in the Cavern, Kore educated himself in the

identification and use of various Human-manufactured weapons. Many nights when he couldn't sleep, he surfed the Internet looking for valuable information.

He discovered such a wealth of information, that he rarely hacked in-to secured sites to get information. The information and location of the U.S. Gold Depository and the Special Forces Headquarters were on the Net.

The M.P.s who shot first and didn't ask questions was a surprise to him; they got the jump on him, and he didn't like that. He had become a control-oriented being; he wanted to shoot first. Nevertheless, Kore was confident that he would always prevail. The Symbios burned that thought into his innermost being---that failure was not an option!

Maj. Gen. Powell sat at his desk. He was in uniform except for his hat. Maj. Gen. Powell was 45 years old, 6-5, built like a lumberjack. He was soft spoken until pissed off. The phone rang; he received word of the break in.

> "What retarded Crack-heads broke into the head-quarters of the Green Berets!" He exclaimed in disbelief. "They need their asses handed to them in a plastic bucket! I'll beat them with a shovel until their dead; I'll kill them slowly with a plastic fork!"

A hundred armed soldiers surrounded the warehouse. Armored vehicles rapidly closed in. Two Apache Helicopters circled the building. Gen. Powell was also there; he wanted blood. When the soldiers went into the warehouse, the only occupant was the downed M.P.s. Creates of weapons were missing.

The next day, Kore and his men dressed in the local clothing. They also had the scarves, with brown and gray wool massoud caps. They entered the cave early. The Special Forces weapons, ammunition and equipment was stacked neatly in the rear of the cave. Several of the crates were opened for inspection.

125 bars of gold, worth an estimated $50,000,000 was stacked at Kore's feet. Sanballat arrived late.

"My friend, I have brought as many prominent leaders as time would permit," Sanballat stated.
"Fifteen influential Warlords in Afghanistan. They have terrorists cells all over the world."
"Your loyalty to the cause is admirable," Kore replied.

The Warlords stared at the gold at Kore's feet. They had never seen so much wealth at one place and time. They walked over, inspected the gold, and then inspected the open crates of weapons.

"You have kept your word," Sanballat said. "These weapons are new, and the best in the world; not the obsolete junk the Russians sell us."
"You must hate the Americans as much as we do," one of the Warlords said, "why else would you go through all this trouble?"
"I don't hate the Americans: I'm an opportunist, a humble broker of worlds; I aspire after world dominance---even their mentality to control the destinies of others; yes--I also need their resources; their military and secular scientific genius, plus their infrastructure, all working for me. With that accomplished, I'll be invincible!"

Kore stopped talking because the warlords looked at him strangely; they thought Kore was crazy. Kore reasoned, their cause was religious, with a mixture of century-old hatred, with envy and jealousy thrown in for zeal; Kore motives were simple: World Domination.

"In a few days, we'll deliver missile systems, antiaircraft guns, radar, armored vehicles and other equipment we took from Ramstein Air Force Base, Germany.

"In six months, we'll deliver aircraft and teach you to fly them; ships and submarines."

Kore didn't mentioned that he had nuclear warheads. He wasn't ready to trust them with those.

"Sanballat, here's $50,000,000 in gold. This is only a down payment. Don't double cross me; there's no place on Earth you can hide. Take everything that's here. Leave nothing, not even an empty crate.

I will also need skilled tradesmen, machine operators and metal workers. Pay them well; swear them to secrecy."

Kore gave Sanballat a communication device.

"Keep me informed. That's all."

The aliens beamed to the Cavern.

CHAPTER FIVE
PRESIDENT GRANT

News of the extraordinary gold heist at the U.S. Depository, the thief at Fort Bragg and Ramstein Bases was the hot topic of the day for the Armed Forces officials.

The news agencies and general public were keep in the dark concerning the alien invasion and the events. The governments of the world thought it prudent to give complete credit for the increase in violence to the terrorists organizations.

The nation was on high alert; the NATO allies were also on alert; all U.S. Bases and embassies tightened security, and the Captains of the Air-craft Carriers awaited orders to sail.

The newly-inaugurated President of the United States, Grant Kensington, demanded a solution.

In Washington D.C., a Meeting of the Joint Chiefs of Staff convened with Five-Star Gen. West. West, Gen. Obama, Gen. Powell, Admiral Bing, Defense Secretary Peace, Marshall of Homeland Security, plus Generals and Admirals were present.

General West was a West Point graduate and the only female among them. She was a heavy-set Black woman with a pretty face; she was 5-8 in height; she wore a long curly weave ponytail.

General Obama was 6 foot tall, skinny and had big ears. He was a light-completed Black man. He's a Christian with a passion for hunting terrorists.

Defense Secretary Peace was a short man who looked like a College Professor or Accountant. He always wore sweaters with patched elbows, always has a pocket guard with ink pens and a calculator.

They have been up all night, which was evident by the empty takeout food containers and empty cups of coffee. They looked tired. The tired Officials have folders in front of them marked "Top Secret."

"America and its allies are on the highest alert. The Alien Kore Threat must be dealt with, "Gen. West told them."

"Praise the Lord for reciprocity: Kore will learn a valuable lesson---that he'll reap what he has sown! Obama added.

"Well put, General," Peace nodded. The C.I.A. file also contains photos of the extraterrestrial named Kore."

"And don't look surprised," Gen. West interjected, "we've known for decades that aliens have visited Earth; some have used Earth as a "weigh station," a place to rest and get repairs done between solar systems; but Alien Kore, as he's called, is the only one who has established a foothold on Earth; he's in Afghanistan and has Moon operations."

"The news agencies are becoming difficult to handle," Defense Sec. Peace added, "this time, we can't lay this level of destruction solely on Sanballat, Al-Queda or the Taliban. They don't have the technology to pull off something like this."

"For decades our enemies had been the Russians and Chinese, then the Human terrorists---and now its alien terrorists," Admiral Bing joined in the conversation.

"My M.P.s at Fort Bragg reported that the assailants wore black military uniforms, body armor with insignia that my men didn't recognize," Gen. Powell stated. "Their weapons were energy based. In the middle of the warehouse floor was a large silver ring platform. That's how they got in and left the scene."

"So they have the ability to transport objects to and from their ship?" Gen. Bing asked.

"Apparently," Gen. Powell continued. "Also, a month ago, an incident report came across my desk. Col. Mack in Uzbekistan, stated that a team of his men, the Pit Bulls, were killed by an unknown heat weapon. We thought it was a dirty bomb; not we know it was the aliens defending local terrorists."

"If the twelve nuclear warheads stolen from Ramstein Base fall into Al-Queda or Taliban hands, the landscape of this nation and the balance of power will be changed forever," Defense Sec. Peace added.

"I don't think Alien Kore is stupid. He wouldn't give nuclear weapons to people who are willing to even blow themselves up; hell, they might blow him up too!"

"Stealing our gold was a personal message," Gen. West added, "Other countries have gold reserves---therefore, we have upgraded the security by moving the New York gold reserves.

"Therein lies their weakness," Admiral Bing suggested, "The theft of gold and weapons are intended to back military operations on Earth; the aliens don't have enough resources---material, weapons or personal---to attack us and win, so they're using our natural and Human resources against us."

An aid to Gen. Obama came into the room and handed him a folder. What he feared was confirmed.

Gen. Obama was a very important man. His duties were to maintain and operate all U.S. nuclear Intercontinental Ballistic Missiles(ICBM), monitor the entire world, launch military and navigational satellites into space, monitor space itself, monitor positions and behaviors of non-U.S. space vehicles and space debris, provide weather information, world-wide communications, missile warnings, and navigational systems to soldiers. Obviously, other agencies assisted in this undertaking: The 90th Space Wing in Wyoming, and the North American Air Defense Command (NORAD) in Cheyenne Mountain, Colorado.

"Our Space-Based Infrared System (SBIRS) of thirty satellites circling the Earth and projecting an electronic shield over America; and our Ground –Based Electro-Optical Deep-Space Surveillance (GEODSS) confirms that at the times and places there was a security breech, was a corresponding electromagnetic disturbance above the Earth. Our conclusion is that an invisible alien spacecraft is in Earth orbit and responsible for all this."

"Thank you General," Gen. West told him, "I must inform the President."

SERIAL KILLER

Jane and her husband Ronald had just finished their workout at the local gym. They lived and worked in New York City. The couple were middle aged and believed they needed to work out at least twice a week, eat better foods and take care of their bodies, if they planned to be around a long time. They were married 15 wonderful years, had three children, and were still very much in love. It was dark when they left the gym and headed towards the car.

> "Honey, do you feel like driving?" Ronald asked. "I think I strained a shoulder muscle. I knew I shouldn't have done that last set of fifteen reps."
> "No problem, muscle man, you're not a twenty-year-old anymore."

As they approached the car, they heard a soft "pop" sound behind them. Both turned around and saw a tall man completely dressed in black leather standing with a large machete raised to strike.

> "Wait!" Ronald fearfully protested.
> "If it's money you want, here, take it." Jane added and threw her purse on the ground in front of the assailant.

But the tall assailant didn't wait. He lowered the machete and chopped Ronald's clean head off; then approached Jane. She was hysterical, but knew she couldn't fight off this giant attacker, who was armed with the most wicked blade she could ever imagine. She took her Pepper Spray from her keychain and sprayed his face; but the assailant, with his fingers, wiped it from his face and licked his fingers.

Swiftly, General Urich killed her too. Then he teleported away. Gen. Urich, a psycho serial killer, was now in London England. After murdering the couple in New York, his fiendish urges weren't satisfied.

He patiently waited in an alley near a busy nightclub. Since being on Earth, this would be his twentieth victim. A young woman in her twenties, left a nightclub. She was alone. She walked haphazardly down the sidewalk; her blue jeans were too tight and her heels taller than she was used too, plus she was tipsy from one drink too many. As she crossed a side street, Gen. Urich grabbed her. He placed his hand over her mouth and dragged her into an alley. She struggled and fought back, but he stabbed her several times then cuts her throat. Satisfied that she was dead, he transports away from the scene.

CAVERN DEFENSES

From a tribal village, Sanballat, the Earth Marshall, distributed gold and weapons to the Warlords. He hired laborers and skilled tradesmen to work in the Cavern. He recruited and trained terrorists in the camps, created terrorists cells in foreign countries, and ordered bombings, assassinations of Judges, Politicians and several government officials who would not cooperate.

When Gen. Urich wasn't out murdering the innocent, he supervised the training and installation of SAM sites, radar stations, antiaircraft guns and other weapon systems positioned throughout the region. Finances and equipment were purchased or stolen on a daily basis, even when attempts to hide these assets was implementted. Very little escaped the scanners and transporting capability of the aliens.

Boris Monday, head of Intelligence, expanded Kore's worldwide influence. He bribed politicians and brokered deals with organized crime syndicates all over the world. The evil effects of the Alien Kore Threat was felt in every major city throughout the world. In massive groups, concerned citizens around the world, marched in the streets in demonstration of the lawlessness. They were keep in the dark about the alien invasion, and their worldwide terrorists campaign.

RELUCTANT

President Kensington was a robust man. He stood at 6-10, a former N.B.A Basketball Player. He had close-cropped red hair and a thin mustache.

He stared at the headlines of the Washington Post: "CITIZENS CALL FOR RESIGNATION OF PRESI-DENT KENSINGTON!"

"I was afraid that things would come to this," President Kensington said to himself. "I'm damned if I do and damned if I don't."

President Kensington was a man of peace. He tried hard all his life to please people. It bothered him when people disapproved with anything he did. He was 40 years old, a young President. He wore a close-cut beard; some said he actually favored a young Ulysses S. Grant. He campaigned promising strong government, fiscal re-

responsibility, tougher gun control laws, and the end to occupying the Middle East. He believed that each country should take care of its own borders against terrorism. Kensington won by a landslide.

But in practice, his predecessors had the right idea: They took the fight to the enemy in their own country, to keep them from arriving on U.S soil. To do this involved some sort of occupation. This strategy worked against the Germans, and the Japanese.

The Red Phone rang. The President picked it up. It was the Prime Minister of Israel.

> "Yes, I understand Prime Minister. But we need to meet and discuss other options. Well...if you'll call your aircraft back to base; give me 24 hours to come up with a another alternative. Yes, you have my word. Good bye."

The President hung up the phone. Now he had to make a decision: His campaign promise realized or or sending in more troops for what could likely be a lengthy deployment in the Middle East.

Gen. West, Sec. Peace, and Homeland Security Marshall arrived to brief the President for the fourth time since the aliens arrived.

> "We cannot withhold our military options any longer, "Gen. West advised the President. "If we withhold our air power, cruise missiles, and ground troops while this so-call Earth Marshall bui-lds a war machine---it would be history repeating itself--- like Adolf Hitler building his

Nazi Germany war machine while the Allies and the entire world watched and waited."

"Don't think that I haven't listened to your reasoning," the President replied. "I believe if we show our hand too soon, the aliens will step in---and who knows what type of arsenal they have. Their weapons might make Sanballat's arsenal look like bows and arrows. At least we know how Sanballat's weapons work, because they're ours."

"Plus we don't know if Kore can call for reinforcements from his world," Sec. Peace added.

"I know---worst case scenario: A fleet of spacecrafts attack us," President Kensington said.

"We haven't been able to reach Kore; he hasn't answered our diplomatic inquiries." Gen. West told him.

"Mr. President "I inclined to agree with Gen. West," Marshall of Homeland Security said."If we don't do something, we'll spend a trillion dollars to guard our borders, and if we don't succeed, we'll be rebuilding the infrastructure of America,"

"Your analysis is duly noted," Pres. Kensington told him.

"My office is working around the clock with the F.B.I. and local law enforcement, "Marshall continued. "We're doing our best to fight the increase of terrorism in America. Recently we foiled plots to blow up one of our nuclear power plants, and the other targets were Hover Dam and two major oil refineries."

"I understand what you're dealing with. Every day on the nightly news the voter watch their cities burn with violence and hatred," Pres. Kensington stated."They're afraid to allow their children to go to school, the corner store, or play in their own yard. The sale of handguns and assault rifles has increased 100%. People are shooting law-abiding citizens and burning their homes because they "look" like terrorists. Isn't that what Sanballat wants---us to turn on each other? Isn't that what terrorism is about---paralyzing the innocent with fear?"

President Kensington paused to collect his thoughts then continued:

"Five minutes ago, the Prime Minister of Israel ordered air strikes against the missile sites and terrorists camps in Afghanistan. They know that Sanballat was behind the recent bombings in Israel. The only way that I could convince him to abort the mission, was to guarantee that the United States would take out Sanballat."

"Politically, if Israel bombed those sites it would inflame the entire Arab world. Our Arab allies are needed for land bases in the middle east," the Secretary added.

"Kore has powerful allies in Congress; but I'm using my Emergency Powers to authorize a limited but concise Police Action against Alien Kore."

They hurried out of the Oval Office. In the hallway, Gen. West whispered: "Thank you Israel." She was ready to kick alien butt.

BORIS BOSS OF BOSSES

Boris Monday, the Director of the League, was in Detroit for a meeting with the Mafia and other Organized Crime Families.

Monday cruised up in a new Lincoln Navigator. His bodyguard drove him. The mansion was heavily guarded with street soldiers who toted machineguns. Men walked the grounds and guarded the vehicles. Two gunmen were on the upper balcony also with machineguns.

Boris climbed the steps with his bodyguard. As he entered into the room men searched them. Their weapons were placed on a table with the others. The table looked like a Gun and Knife Show.

The crime bosses from Detroit, New York City, Chicago, Atlantic City, Los Vegas, and the West Coast were in attendance. These men represented families: Puzo, Geno, Nitty, Bugs and Big Al.

"I'm Boris Monday, representing Alien Kore and the League. I came to make a deal with you."
"Then come on with it. Time is money!" Puzo blurted, disrespectfully.
"Right now, each of you has a portion of a city. You can own the State you live in with our oversight and with our protection."
"What's in it for Alien Kore?" Nitty countered.
"Kore gets 50 percent off the top."
"It's ingenious!" Nitty exclaimed.
"Yes, the United States will soon be on the auction block!" Monday stated with sure utmost certainty.
"Sounds un-American to me," Bugs from Detroit strongly protested. "My parents came from Sicily

By ship in the late 30s; they came through Ellis Island, New York. America embraced them. I believe America deserves better than this."

Nitty was amazed at Puzo's statement.

"Do you want violins to go with that song?" Nitty said sarcastically. "The truth is--- Your father and my father came from the same village; when they got here they were treated like the Negroes; they couldn't speak English so they couldn't get a job; that's when our fathers started the Mafia in America."

"That's not altogether true," Puzo countered.

"Oh, you being a good citizen and all---Do you file Income Taxes each year? No, you're a criminal, like the rest of us. Don't start waving the American flag, when you have drug dealers targeting middle school children! Now, that's un-American!"

Bugs was angry-red faced. If he had a gun he would have shot Nitty in the face. The nerve of Nitty disrespecting him in front of the other bosses.

"I think you've crossed the line," Bugs said to Nitty. "And for you---Boris Monday---you're a different kind of fool. The U.S. Military won't sit on their asses while you take America from them? Aliens or not, the U.S. Military aren't punks!"

"I believed we've gotten sidetracked," Monday said with disappointment.

"I'll contact you with our decision," Geno, the West Coast reprehensive said. We need to see

how you handle the U.S. Armed Forces."
"Fair enough," Monday replied.

Boris handed business cards to everyone. Bugs threw Boris' card on the floor.

"Contact me at this number," Boris told the others.

The mobsters exited the house, walked to the parking area, and climbed into their vehicles. Bug's chauffeur pulled up. Bugs and his bodyguard got in. His vehicle was bulletproof, biohazard-proof and blast-proof.

Gen. Urich in the VXT materialized above Bug's vehicle. He was already there, watching and listening to the meeting via electronics on Monday's body.

A precision energy beam burned a hole through the roof. It also bored a large hole in the top of Bugs' head. The other passengers fled. Like a hot knife in butter, two energy beams cut the car into four large chunks. The gasoline tank exploded with a loud blast and ball of fire. The VXT Tractor Beam picked up the burning pieces and threw them into the swimming pool.

Monday turned to Nitty.

"I will not be disrespected. We can get extreme, dangerously evil if provoked."

CHAPTER SIX
ANAMI KORDOVA

Starship Andromeda, the Flagship of the System Lord Anami Kordova, cruised through space at Warp Factor Ten. This vessel, one of three in the convoy, was heavily armed; yet it was more a ship of peace.

The designation was Earth. They had been in space over six months, with another three months remaining. The ship was enormous; conditions on the ship were comfortable for the 3,000 member crew. The majority of them were native Earth people.

Two sweaty assailants rushed towards Christina. They were big and muscular; their eyes were bloodshot with murder and madness; their swords were long, sharp, the handles held firmly in their hands; they fully expected to see her warm human blood dripping off the razor tips of their weapons. One sliced at her neck to cut off her head but she ducked; the other crouched like a Ninja tiger; he grinned through broken and rotten teeth. He thrust repeatedly at her lower body but only met the clang and sparks flying from her swift blade against his own.

She tumbled on the floor into a forward roll, leaped up and kicked the sword out of the first assailant's hand; when she landed on her feet, she kicked the attacker in the groin, then another kick broke his leg; then she ran him through the mid section with a quick flick of her sword. The other man charged her. It seemed that he was angrier than the first. She waited until he was close then forcefully threw her sword through his neck.

She smiled and walked away in victory. Then, she heard a sound; the assailant wasn't dead. She quickly turned around in time to see his hand fumble for a dagger. She reached in her belt and withdrew two of her own daggers. She threw them together: The daggers stuck the assailant in both eyes; this time he was dead.

"The simulation is over," Barbara AB-E-5, Christina's personal body guard said. Barbara was an Artificial Intelligence being assigned to protect Christina and give her combat training.

"Did I pass the test?" Christina asked hopefully.

Another large being appeared. It was completely clad in sleek black body armor. Embedded in its head was a diamond-shaped crystal that glowed white and then red.

"You're not done until you defeated me!"
"Not fair Anami. I can't fight you in your System Lord pajamas!"
"Pajamas? I'd have you to know that this magnificent weapon has been used by the last five System Lords. And no System Lord has ever been defeated while wearing this weapon system."
"Take it off and I'll kick your butt," she joked."
"Some other time; Anyway, No System Lord has been defeated by his wife either!"
"Does that include Queen Wench-Desiree?"
"I don't believe that she ever had a husband---she's too---contrary, as we say. But I watched the entire fight. I would be honored to fight beside you, and that's a whole lot safer."
"But you did finish the exercise in record time,"

Barbara stated.

"I made a mistake; I assumed Assailant #2 was dead but he wasn't."

"Hundreds of recruits have made the error of assuming an opponent was dead because of his wounds; logically thinking, he should be dead; but many humanoid and reptile species have redundant systems or the ability to regenerate damaged organs; such beings would have to be completely destroyed by phaser blast.

The body armor disappeared off of Anami.

"Where did the suit go?" Christina asked.

"It's still with me. You can't see it because it's in a different dimension, out-of-phase with the material universe. I can make it materialize at will."

"Where did it come from?"

"Long ago one of our System Lords rescued the daughter of a System Lord in the Delta Quadrant; she was abducted out of revenge and would have been executed.. In return, our System Lord was given this special suit---now, let's go get something to eat."

After lunch, they went to the Bridge.

URIDIAN BEAUTY

Anami met with his Starship Officers: Captain Elizabeth Harmony, of the Andromeda, the Flagship of the Centaurus Empire; Commander Ben Hur of the Nova; and Captain. Ezar of the Shallum.

The three Starships traveled in a triangular pattern,

with the Starship Andromeda leading the charge. The Empire Starship was a space-going city. It was 4,500 ft. long and 10 deck-levels thick. It housed nearly 4,000 troops and crew members; it held 50 Interceptors and 10 Shuttles; it sported multi-directional missile launchers, 24 Gatling-type proton-plasma cannon stations, cloaking, tractor beams, and other defensive weaponry. It was the largest ship known in Centaurus. The Empire had 200 Starships.

Captain Harmony was an Uridian: Blue skinned with silky white hair. She was 200 years old, but looked about 35 in Human years. Captain Harmony was gorgeous by galactic standards. She was the first of her species to Captain an Empire Starship, and the first to Captain Andromeda, the "Air Force One" of Centaurus.

"All is well on the horizon," Capt. Harmony reported to Anami.

"All system functioning within acceptable perimeters on all Starships."

"Very well," Anami replied.

"Christina, do you think the Humans on Earth will find me attractive?"

"I think you know the answer to that: For years you dated a handsome Texan named Rusty Meyers."

"Yeah…but all he talked about was getting back home to the cattle ranch. I believe he loved those stupid cows more than me!"

"He was only home sick. I'm sure he appreciated your company."

"Well, I heard he's on one of the ships. He probably can't wait to get to the ranch and "punch the a cows"

"I don't think they actually punch them with their fists," Christina laughed, "it means they lead them from place to place."

"Oh…"

"Don't let me interrupt your conversation. I'll watch the Bridge, and let you too catch up. "

"Thanks Boss," Christina kissed him. She and Capt. Harmony left the Bridge.

THE STARGATE

While Sanballat was spreading terrorism throughout the world, and Boris Monday was selling pieces of America to the highest bidder, in the Cavern, Kore was hard at work managing the factory that was building VXT Interceptors. Kore utilized the Androids, robots, and Human labor; Kore's Supervisors were his own people. Kore used industrial duplicating and replicating machines, plus the train car stockpile of dismantled Mu Galaxy-Class Cruiser parts, and Interceptor parts from the captured and dismantled Mutant Gray ships.

He had warp drive engines, control panels, computers, weapon systems and other secondary systems already built; he just had to build ships to put it all in. The two Cruiser hulls that he was building were on the moon; this project was too big for the Cavern. Key components were manufactured and assembled in the Cavern, then transported to the Moon. On the Moon, he had an oxygen-gravity environment base constructed; outside of the base Android and robot welders fabricated the outer hull and rooms inside the Cruisers. Special alloys not found on Earth were extracted from one of the nine planets or Moons, and used in the construction of the VXT and the Mu Cruiser.

Expansion of the Cavern was a twenty-four hour project. The Humans blasted and created new rooms every day. The Cavern became a subterranean city with housing units. The Human workers, once in the Cavern, weren't allowed to leave until their off day; and since they were transported in and out, they didn't know the whereabouts of the Cavern.

A large room contained the electrical power generator, Life-Support and Shield Generator. Another room had the Stargate in it.

Kore's Moon Base, located in a large crater, had a transparent dome that covered the entire crater. Human, Centaurus, androids and robot welders worked on a Mu Galaxy-Class Cruiser from the salvaged engines and components of the Space Train and other Earth materials.

In the Stargate Room, Dr Q worked feverishly on the Stargate. It took a lot of power to operate it. He used Zed-EM Crystals from his home world. His Mutant Assistants downloaded star chart computations to program the MG-Console to locate and record all the planet addresses in the Milky Way Galaxy---including the Mu Worlds and Chud Worlds (Those worlds belonging to the Ruler).

In the Stargate Room, the Stargate stood erect. It was a large oval metal doorway. From the Cavern-side was seen the terrain at the destination, as though looking out a window or door of a house. There were Power cables attach to it; a computer con-sole was also connected.

The sliding door opened and Kore walked into the room. Dr. Q and his faithful assistants, four Mutant Grays, also worked on the Stargate.

"Is it operational?" Kore asked.
"To answer that question, I need a test subject."
"Don't look at me. Send one of your Grays through it."
"They're too valuable."

Kore leaves the room and returns with a Human assembly line worker.

"Not so valuable, uh?" Kore shrugged.

The man trembled and objected. Kore shoved him into the energized Stargate. Seconds later, the worker came back unharmed.

"It's ready," Dr. Q announced.
"Thanks for volunteering," Kore said to the worker.

Feeling generous, Kore handed him a stack of hundred dollar bills totaling ten thousand dollars.

"Hazardous Duty Pay. Don't tell anyone about this machine or the gray creatures," Kore told him.
"My lips are sealed. And thanks for the money."

The laborer rejoined his fellow workers. He was shaken, urinated on himself a bit, but was otherwise unharmed.

"I saw five gray devils," he said.

"Brother, you mean white devils---Americans?"

"No, they were little gray monsters with big heads and charcoals eyes. Kore keeps them locked in the back room so they can't eat us!"

"Brother, you must sleep more at night, so you won't dream while you're awake. There are no gray monsters down here."

While in the Stargate Room, shooting pain gripped Kore. He grabbed his head; he clutched the console to keep from falling.

"What's wrong?"

"The Symbios won't stop talking. Sometimes I think my head will explode."

"What's it saying?"

"It Keeps ordering me to kill Faye. Are you sure this thing can't be removed?

"The Spawn of the Ruler of Chud has never been successfully removed; all have died a excruciating death."

"If I didn't need you, I'd kill you for doing this to me."

"You can't kill me. The Symbios won't let you. So find someone else to threaten!"

Kore left the room. He didn't want to hear Dr. Q's voice for a while. For the most part, he didn't trust Dr. Q to tell him the truth anyway. In his quarters, Kore took several pills for the head pain. The pain immediately subsided.

"Let's go out," Kore said to Faye Kordova. "Where---Kabul? Got too much beauty and booty to hide behind a burke."

"No, it's a surprise.

The couple and two bodyguards transported to Paris, France. It was Springtime and the flowers were bloomed. Perfume fragrances were in the air. They rode in a limousine for a while, then walked the streets of Paris. They held hands. They looked like millions of people who had ever fallen in love with Paris.

Kore took Faye to several of the tourist sites. She also went shopping at the most expensive stores in Paris. She bought Jewelry, shoes, purses, perfumes, hair pieces, makeup, and many other female beauty products. Kore also bought cases of wine, and a few cases of his favorite Crown Royal Whiskey. He stuffed it all in the limousine.

"Are you tired yet?" Kore asked hopefully.
"No, just getting started."
"Okay, Fabulous Faye Futura."
"And don't you forget it, mister!"
"But we're married; you're a Kordova."
"I know, it takes a while to get used to."

The bodyguards stayed at a reasonable distance. They were amazed at the effect Faye had on Kore. She kept the mean Symbios from surfacing, by keeping another part of Kore---love in his heart alive.

Kore actually laughed at her jokes; laughing was something Kore seldom did; he was lost without her. The evil that he did, he was careful not to do it around her. She brought out the best in him, the old Kore Kordova, the romantic.

They found a nice cafe'. The sound of classical music played. Kore and Faye sat together; the bodyguards sat at a distance. The waiter brought menus, wine lists and bread to them.

"I need to freshen up."
"Take your time."

With her usual sexy walk, Faye strutted to the rest room. Several men, and two lesbians, admired her physique. Kore shook his head and read the menu. Faye came back. Kore motioned to the waiter.

"Excuse me," Kore began, "what is chicken---is it a delicacy?"

The waiter looked at him strangely. He didn't want to say the wrong thing, because Kore was well dressed and could have been a Mafia Don.

Since Kore spoke perfect French, the waiter assumed that he was high on medication. In fact, Kore learned several languages since being on Earth; but he didn't spend any time researching restaurants and food; he just ate what he saw others eat or what looked good to eat or drink. Most of the time he ate on the ship.!

"No sir, chicken is a very common meat, but is served in many ways; how would you like it?"
"Let me order dear," Faye offered. "I believe I know more about fine foods than you do."

After a hardy meal, they left the café'. As Kore and Faye walked close together, hand-in-hand, they disappeared. By-standers were amazed! Bodyguards transported the limousine and everything they bought to the Cavern.

OPERATION GREATNESS

One of the U.S. Space Wing's secret assets for protecting America proved valuable in revealing the whereabouts of Alien Kore's headquarters. This was discovered when the Think Tank experimented with a device salvaged from the 1960 downed Mu Galaxy Cruiser. For some reason, it lost power and crashed in the Nevada desert. The wreckage was stored at Area 51.

They engineered this unit with an magnetic field evaluator plus ground-penetrating sonar, connected to the U.S. Space Wing's orbiting satellites and tracking system. From this combination of alien and Human technology emerged the outline of the cloaked Heavy Metal, and also detected the presence of the Shield Generator, and the recent activations of the Stargate.

They knew the Cavern wasn't far from where the "Bulldog" Special Forces Team was ambushed. This information was quickly forwarded to General West and the Joint Chiefs.

Congress was briefed on the crisis; the nation was placed on the highest alert. The allies were informed: Operation Greatness was a Green Light.

The Strategic Air Command (SAC) readied the Intercontinental Ballistic Missiles (ICBM) for launch from their silos located in Nebraska and the Midwest United States. Air Combat Command based at Langley Air Force Base, Virginia, was the largest and most important of the Commands. It operated all the United States Air Force's 1,700 combat aircrafts.

Two E-3 Sentry AWAC surveillance planes monit-

Ored and transmitted live images to Forward Operations located at Bagnam Airfield, north of Kabul. These planes crisscrossed Afghanistan and mapped the coordinates of the 2,000 SAM missile launchers, 2100 radar stations, 1800 antiaircraft guns, 1500 artillery and armored vehicles, and hundreds of .30-50 caliber machine gun emplacements.

There were also a staggering seventy terrorists camps, villages and cave fortifications to keep track of.

The E-3 Sentry was a converted Boeing 707. It had a 30-ft. radar dome on top of the fuselage; it was designed with probing, long-range surveillance technology; enemy ships, structures, vehicles and aircrafts were seen for 250 sq. miles from 9 miles above; it used the Global Positioning System (GPS) and military satellites of the U.S. Space Command.

In secret, on a U.S. Military base, five B-2 Spirits rolled onto the tarmac. They were: The Spirit of America, Spirit of Arizona, Spirit of New York, Spirit of Indiana, and the Spirit of Ohio. The B-2 stealth bomber looked like a mechanical bat. It was designed to fly high, fast, and undetected. Its exterior space age design, made of non-radar absorbing materials, and its unique shape, made it invisible to radar; and therefore it was unlikely to get shot down by SAMs, antiaircraft guns or enemy fighters.

The power plant for the B-2 was 4 General Electric F-118-GE-100 non-afterburning turbofans; its maximum speed was Mach 0.95, 604 M.P.H; its cruising speed 541 M.P.H; its flight range was 6,000 miles, with a service ceiling of 50,000 ft. It was equipped with two internal bays for 50,000 lbs. of ordinance. The price for the B-2 was one billion dollars each. For this mission, each carried sixteen B83 nuclear missiles.

From Whiteman Air Force Base in Missouri, fifteen Boeing B-52 Stratofortresses rolled slowly onto the tarmac. They were huge planes with massive wingspans. The B-52 Stratofortress was a high-altitude bomber. It carried 69, 996 lbs. of bombs. It could "carpet bomb" and destroy a square mile of terrain by dropping 50,000 lbs. of bombs in a single pass. These planes would fly non-stop all the way to Afghanistan, and join in with other B-52s stationed in Germany, plus nine B1B Lancer Bombers, and four KC-135 Stratotanker Fuelers; from Garcia Air Base near the Indian Ocean.

Operation Greatness also consisted of four Fighter Wings of nearly 300 aircrafts: F-15A Eagles, F-16 Fighting Falcons, F-18 Hornets, F-111s, and other effective aircrafts: A-10 Thunderbolt "Wart Hogs", and AC-130 Sprectre Gunships, were fueled and loaded with ordinance at various bases.

The Hindu Kush Mountains wasn't jungle, desert, or bamboo huts---or even the best concrete bunker; these mountains were solid billion-year-old volcanic rock. This massive firepower was assembled to destroy an enemy hiding beneath 50-5,000 ft. of solid rock. Though Afghanistan was a land-locked country, the U.S. Navy would play a vital role in the extermination of the insect named Sanballat Hadad: The Earth Marshall.

The U.S. Navy had battle fleets located throughout the world. The 2nd Fleet operated in the Atlantic Ocean; 3rd Fleet in the Central Pacific Ocean; 5th Fleet stationed at Bahrain, Persian Gulf; 6th Fleet in Naples, Italy for the Mediterranean Sea; and 7th Fleet from Yokosuka, Japan for the Western Pacific and Indian Oceans. The U.S. Navy had 8 Nimitz-Class Aircraft Carriers. Each Carrier was 1,099 ft. long, with a flight deck spanning 252 ft; two nuclear reactors powered it; it carried 85 aircrafts and 3,000 crew, an aircrew of 2,480. The Nimitz-Class Aircraft Carriers launched Tomahawk Cruise Missiles and Trident long-range missiles that could carry nuclear warheads; its range was 4,500 miles at speeds reaching 13,500 M.P.H. These missiles would easily reach their targets.

Surrounding the Carriers were other ships, like the USS Bunker Hill. These ships were equipped with the Aegis (protect) radar system. The system used sound waves to protect surface ships against enemy missile attacks. These anti-missile missiles can shoot down enemy planes and missiles. The escorts were needed to protect the large and slower Aircraft Carriers.

In total, four Carrier Groups and three Nuclear Submarines were designated for Operation Greatness. The rest were needed to protect the homeland and other U.S. Interest.

The North Atlantic Treaty Organization (NATO) also assembled its fleet and made ready to wage war. These countries joined in because they knew this would be the only opportunity to hit Sanballat and the aliens with such overwhelming firepower; strength in numbers was the best defense and also the best offense. They knew it wise to come big or not at all.

China and the Soviet Union, though not a part of NA-

TO, launched their Carriers to meet with the NATO forces at the Indian Ocean. This was the first time since World War II that these two countries fought side-by-side. In modern times, they sided with whomever the U.S. was at war with. But the world had drastically changed, and drastic changes required drastic measures and solutions: they had to beat Alien Kore or join him. Neither the Russians or the Chinese wanted aliens---or anyone else telling them what to do.

Not only were the soldier's lives on the line but the lives of those they loved and loved them; even the lives of people in foreign lands, depended on this victory.

CHAPTER SEVEN
TOO MUCH TOO SOON

Kore and Gen. Urich were on the Bridge of the Heavy Metal. On the view screen, they saw the Coalition Forces, and other nations on their way to the Middle East to attack him.

"I pushed them a little too hard." Kore concluded. "We need another week to finish the Mu Galaxy Cruiser, and a few VXT Interceptors."

"The only complete one we had was dismantled to fabricate its parts. It would take days to just put that one back together," Gen. Urich replied."

"Tell my Earth Marshall to hire a hundred more laborers."

"We're already running three shifts," Scarface told him.

"I know. Set up more assembly lines in the vacant rooms."

"I have an idea that will give us the time we need," Gen. Urich suggested.

"Go, do whatever it takes."

HOSTAGES

Commander General Perry was the NATO Supreme Commander. He was stationed in Brussels, Germany. He sat at his desk and signed documents. Comdr. Gen. Perry was a British Officer. He was 5-10, in his early fifties, with a military haircut. He had a pipe in his mouth but seldom lit it because he was trying to quit smoking. General Urich and two Elite Guardsmen materialize in his office.

> "Come with me, General."
> "Have I a choice in the matter?
> "No, you don't."

The Guards transported Comdr. Gen. Perry to the Cavern. Next, Gen. Urich and his guards traveled to Tokyo, Japan to kidnap President Soto. They materialize outside Soto's bedroom; his bodyguards responded, and the Elites killed both of them. Pres. Soto and his wife, Akiko, were asleep in bed. Soto awakened when the bodyguards fell. Gen. Urich and the Elites opened the bedroom door and walked into the room.

> "Get dressed. Kore is waiting."
> "What's the meaning of this? Do you know who I am?"
> "Yes, we do, that's why we're here."

Soto's wife got out of bed. She grabbed a baseball bat and waved it threatening.
> "I know how to use this. Get out of our bedroom!"
> "Not long ago, I threw an old man---about your age--- out an airlock into outer space."

Akiko dropped the ball bat. They transport her husband away. This time, Gen. Urich was in Rome Italy. The target was Italian President, Bruno Bogotto. Pres. Bogotto was taking a shower with his 20-year-old mistress employed as a maid.

Pres. Bogotto was a short and chubby man in his 60s.

His mistress was Asian and gorgeous. She was 5-2 with large breast. Her black and white uniform was hanging on the towel rack.

Gen. Urich and Elites appeared outside the bathroom. They entered the bathroom. Pres. Bogotto heard the door open, but couldn't see who it was because the shower glass was steamed up. Nervously, he whispered:

> "It's my wife. She's back early from visiting her relatives.
> "Does she own a gun?"
> "I do," Gen. Urich replied. "You're lucky that it's me and not your wife. Kore wants to see you."
> "Why? I'm only a peasant who the people made their President."
> "I enjoy killing people, so Kore made me a General; don't despise small beginnings."
> "I'll be quiet now."

Pres. Bogotto got dressed. He straightened the toupee on his head.

Gen. Urich tossed a towel to the maid. He winked at her; in his heart he wanted to butcher her, but there wasn't time. The Elites transported Pres. Bogotto.

President Kensington was late for a meeting. The Secret Service Agents walked him and Vice-President Reed to different limousines. For National Security purposes, the President and Vice-President never traveled together; if tragedy struck it wouldn't take out both of them, thus leaving America without a leader.

> "Hold on, I forgot some papers," the President said, "I left them on my desk. I'll be back in a minute."

It wasn't like Kensington to leave important papers on his desk; but he had a lot on his mind. Though he believed that everyone in Housekeeping was honest, it wasn't responsible behavior for the Commander-in-Chief to leave Top Secret documents laying around.

Vice-President Reed stepped out of the White House. Through a different exit. Three Secret Service Agents were with her, and several stood around the black limousine. Vice President Reed was a Caucasian Woman in her 40s. She was 5-7, brunette with blue eyes.

Gen. Urich and twelve Elites appeared near them. The Secret Service responded with their 9mm pistols. One Agent reached under the seat and brought out a machinegun. He fired on the aliens.

Agent Brisco of the Secret Service threw a smoke grenade. He leveled his 9mm and killed three of the Elites, with head shots. The other agents aimed at the bodies and the bullets bounce off their armor.

Gen. Urich killed Agent Brisco and two other Secret Service Agents. Three White House Police Officers arrived on the scene. Soon after arrival, they were wounded in the battle. Dead Agents and Police Officers lay on the concrete and grassy area. Sirens from the White House Police and Washington Police forces approached the Main Gate of the White House.

President Kensington returned to the side door where the limousines were parked. He heard the gunfire and knew there was trouble. From his vantage point behind a pillar, he saw Urich and the Elites: He also saw Secret Service Agents laying on the White House lawn;

they were wounded and some were dead; the drivers of the limousines were down on the pavement.

President Kensington hid near the doorway and listened.

> "Where's President Kensington?" Gen. Urich questioned Vice-Pres. Reed.
> "California."
> "Liar. I should kill you."
> "Then search the entire White House; it's only 132 rooms, 35 bathrooms, and six levels."
> "You're a Human encyclopedia. No time to search. You'll do."

The Elites transported Vice-Pres. Reed to the Cavern. The dead Elite Soldiers were also transported. President Kensington was safe.

Kore, Gen. Urich, Sanballat, the kidnapped Presidents, NATO Comdr. and the U.S. Vice Pres. were in a large room. Video Equipment for a satellite up-feed was visible and ready to go.

Sanballat, in his Earth Marshall uniform, stood next to Kore. The hostages are shown. Kore began the live broadcast all over the world.

> "I am Alien Kore from the Centaurus Constellation. I am now your System Lord. A Coalition Fleet is on its way to topple my regime. This would not be in your best interest."

> "You have seventy-two hours to reconsider and return to your bases, or these Leaders will be executed." He showed the hostages.

The uplink was terminated.

"Are you going to kill us?" Pres. Bogotto asked.

"It could come to that," Kore replied unmoved.

"Let's negotiate a truce," Vice-Pres. Reed suggested.

"Why bargain with me unless the governments of the world are ready to surrender to me?"

"A truce would eliminate the bloodshed on both sides. Peace with honor," Vice-Pres. Reed assured him.   .

"My middle name is bloodshed; somewhere in your writings, is the statement "There's no peace for the wicked." I have no need for honor. All I've got is vision and ambition."

"Consider this: The Coalition retreats. You'll get an island-nation with U.N. Membership."

"I see why Kensington made you Vice-President; you think on your feet. However, I decline your ridiculous offer. Resistance is Futile---that's my motto."

Faye quietly came into the room. She was aware of the recent events; she watched a lot of television.

Although she was always absent when Kore conducted business, she felt sorry that the Officials got caught up in this crisis. She gave the hostages food and refreshments, then went back to her quarters.

Kore came into the room. Faye was crying. He'd hadn't seen her cry before. He was touched.

"What's wrong Faye?"

"Those nice people are going to die."

"Why do you say that; the President of the United States can save them."

"I have a feeling---he won't---and you're going to kill them."

"Stay out of this Faye. This isn't something you need to be concerned with. I came here to be System Lord by whatever means necessary! Take your puppy for a walk or something.

"The News Commentators say that the U.S. Policy won't allow the President to even negotiate with you; this isn't like Centaurus.

"Faye, again, stay out of this!"

Kore's workers hastened to finish the VXT Interceptors. The Mu Galaxy-Class Cruiser were almost ready to test the engines. But Coalition Forces approached the Arabian Sea. The deadline ended. A video message arrived at Kore's headquarters.

"President Kensington: To Alien Kore: The NATO consensus stands: We won't negotiate with terrorists.

The cameraman pointed the camera towards Kore and the hostages; and the uplink was established. Kore took his weapon out. He leveled it at the hostages and squeezed the trigger: they disappeared. Sanballat pulled out a big sword.

"I wanted to behead them!" Sanballat whispered.

"What does it matter---they're gone," Kore told him. Do your beheading outside of my Cavern.

The video camera turned back to Kore.

"To everyone who watched this execution and have soldiers on the way here----dig plenty of graves, because I guarantee you'll fill them up!"

Millions of people around the world saw the video of Kore executing the hostages; they were horrified. But there were also millions who applauded Kore, those who had vowed to serve him in his New World Order.

THE MOTHER OF ALL BATTLES

The World Wars were mostly fought on the ground by men with rifles and a few hand grenades. There were also automatic machine guns, mortars, tanks and artillery pieces. The bombers dropped "dumb" bombs, and the fighters dog-fought in the skies above, in an attempt to shoot down the bombers. Hundreds of people died in the air and tens of thousands on the beaches and in the cities of foreign lands. This was done to preserve freedom.

Then the age of advanced technology arrived; freedom still needed to be preserved. Millions were killed by two atomic blasts; and no one had to look into the faces of the people it fell on; they were vaporized, burned or hideously disfigured; and later their children were born with genetic deformities or stillbirth due to the massive energy/radiation release of the split atom. And so, the general conscience became that nuclear weapons was a last not first resort.

Yet to preserve freedom from those who would take it, some perish in order that others may live; the evil must be overcome by the good; the unrighteous evil must not be permitted to triumph over the righteous good; it's the age-old question: Are the lives of the many more precious than the lives of the few? Are some deaths an acceptable, and necessary good?

The President of the United States gave a State of the Union address from a secret location.

> "I encouraged the American people and citizens abroad to stand fast to the freedom principles that made the Human Civilization great; and to defend our dignity as a Race, with the inalienable right to exist in piece without an Overlord! I declare the upcoming Police Action as being a "Just and Righteous Cause," that will go down in history as our "Finest Hour, and the Mother of All Battles! May God bless America and the entire Human Race."

The Indian Ocean was calm; the wind was also calm. The Task Force maneuvered into the Arabian Sea. Carrier Groups that included the USS Enterprise, Coral Sea, and British Carriers of the NATO Alliance were positioned. Russian, Chinese Carriers and Battleships cruised into pre-planned positions. Allied airfields in Turkey, Iraq, Uzbekistan, Bahrain and others stood ready. The Soviet bases were also ready to strike. This was Judgment Day, the moment of truth.

On the Arabian Sea, the U.S.S. Enterprise fired Tomahawk Cruise Missiles over Pakistan to get to the land-locked country of Afghanistan. The other U.S. Carriers followed suit, until a continuous line of guided missiles soared over and between the jagged mountain peaks, then slammed into the seventy alien-operated bases. The crewmen on the Carriers worked in shifts around the clock, as tons of ordinance came up on the elevators and into the launchers. The Russian and Chinese Carriers also delivered their ordinance to their targets.

The alien and Human terrorists fired the antiaircraft guns, field guns and heavy machine guns at the onslaught of cruise missiles. Several of the Cruise Missiles were brought down but the majority of them hit the bases.

The B-52 Bombers arrived. The bomb bay doors opened. Like a long ammunition belt, they dropped thousands of bombs. All seventy bases were hit. The carpet bombing continued throughout the day and night; the B-52s also dropped bombs in the other countries too. There were enough Allied and associated military might to sustain continuous raids throughout the night.

The mountains quaked; a rolling firestorm swept the mountains. It consumed everything in its path. The terrorists hid deep in the caves and underground passageways. They had constructed bomb shelters during the Soviet occupation; yet many didn't go deep enough, because a ground zero blast sucked the air from the caves and the heat vaporized the occupants.

Though the hell was being bombed out of them, they protected their weapons to use against the aircrafts. Hidden in bunkers were the rest of the SAMs and antiaircraft guns.

The next morning the missiles ceased. Each Carrier took its turn and launched their aircrafts. An entire day, the aircrafts destroyed targets then returned to their Carriers. The terrorists targeted the aircrafts, and brought thirty of them down the first day of the airstrike;

they also damage another sixty.

However, considering there were hundreds of aircrafts in the sky all over the mountains, deserts and remote places away from the cities, that many hit was expected. According to the Russians, SAMs and anti-aircraft guns were spotted by their fighter jets; they bombed a mosque, elementary school, hospital and several villages; on their way back they "accidentally" shot down two NATO planes. Those pilots were grounded pending a full investigation.

The AWAC plane patrolling the area picked up radar signatures. The B-1B Lancer Bombers released guided missiles and destroyed the hidden SAM sites and radars installations.

An MC-130 heavy cargo transport that could lift 291,000 lbs. was quickly loaded with a BLU-82 15,000 lb. bomb. This type of bomb was originally developed to create areas for bases and helicopter landing zones in the dense jungle of Viet Nam. The weapon consisted of a metal container filled with 12,600 lbs. of jellied explosive. Because of its size, it was mounted on a palette, then pushed out the rear of a MC-130 Transport. When it hit the ground, the explosion was so tremendous that everything within a diameter of 1,800 ft. was vaporized. It was the next best thing to an atomic bomb, with no radiation.

Under fighter escort, a MC-130 Transport Plane circled above the Cavern. It carries a BLU-82 Weapon strapped to a metal palette on wheels.

Airmen George and Eric readied the weapon.

"One Shock and Awe coming up!" George yelled to Eric above the plane engines.

"Special delivery from the U.S Air Force!" Eric added.

The rear door opened; the Green Light came on. The soldiers pushed the weapon out the door.

DIRECT HIT!

Everything was peaceful in the Cavern. The work was getting done. The minute vibrations of distant explosions was felt but not heard. Everyone knew the Coalition began their bombing campaign. They weren't concerned, because they were safe in the mile-deep Cavern. All they actually heard was the dull hum of electronic devices, and the noises of manufacturing.

Faye was bored in the Cavern, so she got her toenail polish and polished her toenails red. While she polished, she watched the Wendy Williams Show; it was her favorite daytime Talk Show.

The Cavern shifted violently. A steel cross beam fell and hit her on the head. She struggled and got to her feet. She took a few steps and collapsed to the floor. Blood pooled around her head.

Sections of the Cavern collapsed. Chunks of rock fell from the ceiling and smashed machinery. Boulders killed and injures several assembly line workers. VXT components were also destroyed. Electrical fires started; they were quickly extinguished by Kore, Gen Urich and others. The Electric Power Plant went down; emergency flood lights came on. Areas of the Cavern were dark. Confusion and panic erupted as fearful Afghan workers looked for places to hide.

Kore rushed to check on Faye. He entered his room.

He saw Faye on the floor. She was dead. Chloe, her little dog barked madly.

"No!" He cried, not being able to believe his eyes. "This can't happen!"

The only thing good in his life laid motionless on the floor. A deep emptiness came upon him and overtook his soul; then the spirit of agony ripped at his heart. His heart stopped beating in his chest; he was like a dead man walking, a zombie without her; she was the life that he was missing; the hope deferred until he could find his own soul and live again.

Kore knelt over Faye. He picked her up in his arms and held her close. Her blood was on the front of his clothes. He gently laid her on the bed. He sat on the floor to keep from falling onto it.

Gored by rage more than demonic, he pounded his fist on the floor until bloodied. He swore in his heart to eliminate--- with extreme prejudice--- the cause of so much wretchedness. Panic steeped in madness seized him; his lower lip dropped and twisted; his jaw was hard. The tormenting Symbios laughed in his head.

"Shut up---you monster!" Kore yelled at the heckling Symbios.

Tears streamed down his tortured face. He had not cried since being a child.

"Faye, see what those "nice people" did to you?!

Gen. Urich and Dora, an alien came into the room.

"General, gather the Heavy Metal crew: We're

fighting back, Kore said. "And Dora, see to it that Faye is in a safe place in the Cavern. Take care of Chloe too."

"Yes, Sri," she replied.

THE HEAVY METAL

Immediately, Kore transported. He brought the Heavy Metal into a fixed orbit above the Coalition Forces in the Arabian Sea. It was a cloudless day. In clear view were the Carriers and Battleships. Aircrafts came and went from the Carriers.

"Charge all phaser banks; ready missile tubes 1-10. Fire!"

The Heavy Metal materialized. A wide spread pattern of twelve proton missiles, red in color, sped towards the ships below; it was immediately followed by another spread of twelve missiles. After that, the Forward phasers targeted the Coalition vessels.

Alarms sounded on the Carriers and Battleships. The sailors prepared the vessels for impact by closing hatches and compartments; the fire department and medical staff readied; the anti-aircraft guns and turret guns on the battleships fired at the descending missiles; the Gatling Guns spat thousands of bullets into the air, as the antiaircraft gunners blanketed the sky with flack and exploding shells. The USS Bunker Hill and other NATO escorts fired anti-missile missiles at the proton missiles. The Agegis radar system, equipped only on the U.S. and NATO ships, locked onto the missiles and intercepted most of them.

The Russian and Chinese had similar anti-missile missile systems. But three Russian Carriers and two Chinese Carriers received deck hits from proton missiles. Twelve other ships from both countries were also severely damaged by phaser blasts. The Carriers exploded and sank; the Battleships took on water and rolled over on their sides; then descended stern first. The sailors abandoned ship.

The Bunker Hill intercepted and destroyed several of the proton missiles, but couldn't lock on to phaser energy. Therefore, several U.S. Battleships and NATO Battleships, including the Bunker Hill were severely damaged by the aliens. Without help from the Battleships, the Carriers were sitting ducks.

A missile hit the flight deck of the Carrier Enterprise. The blast ripped through the flight deck like the deck was made of cardboard. It blew a gigantic hole through every level of the Enterprise. The magazines of stored ordinance exploded and ripped a gaping hole out her side; secondary explosions from aircrafts and jet fuel added to her demise; then the twin nuclear reactors went critical and the Carrier exploded and went down. Half the crew made it to safety.

Another proton missile hit the Carrier Coral Sea. The missile hit the Control Room, and sheared off the radar towers and a large portion of the middle of the ship. The impact disintegrated the Control Room and blew the aircrafts that were being refueled and loaded with ordinance off the deck into the sea. The damage was also extensive; fire and secondary explosions crippled her; she took on water and also sank.

Kore with bloody knuckles, clutched the arms of his

chair. He was well pleased when a ship sank. His usual Symbios eye glow was pronounced. He wore a fixed insane grin. Then the weapons ceased to operate.

"What's wrong? We got them where we want them!"
"The Phaser Banks and Missile Launchers have overloaded. They will reset in a few minutes.
"I guess the Humans aren't going anywhere. Slow moving vehicles is all they have. Somebody, get me a glass of Whiskey on ice. Destroying an army makes me thirsty!"

His drink was brought to him. Kore sipped it and relaxed a little. He had acquired a taste for Crown Royal. Kore planned to finish off the Coalition. They killed his wife and he wasn't done with them yet---not until the last ship was at the bottom of the ocean.

"Three aircrafts approach, but are Trams (miles) away."
"Shields up. Back Away at one-third Impulse," Kore ordered.
"Shields are at fifty percent; Impulse Engines are sluggish but responding."
"Let them come: The materials the Humans make their aircrafts from can't withstand the intensity of a Tractor Beam pulling on them."
"But we have to conserve energy until the weapons reset. I think cloaking would be our best option."
"Make it so."

Three B-2 Spirits stealth fighters arrived in the upper atmosphere several miles away and below the ship.

Col. Lacy piloted the Spirit Ohio.

"Red Dog to Dark Wing: Switching over to NORAD Tracking. Arming weapons."

Col. Lacy lifted the switch covers, flipped two switches and armed the nuclear missiles.

"Executive Order, Apha-359226," General. West radioed him and the other pilots."
"Confirmed: Alpha-359226."

The B-2s flew in an arrowhead formation. They climbed to the stratosphere. Each pilot released a nuclear missile. All three hit the Heavy Metal. The flash and explosion was tremendously bright. The shields failed. The exterior of the ship was melted and ripped away; the external weapons melted. Warped metal and jagged holes dotted the hull. Hull plating detached and floated in outer space. Twelve crewmembers suffocated in outer space. Kore got off the floor. He wasn't hurt but stunned. None of the Bridge Crew were injured.

"Damage report! Kore demanded.
"Hull severely damaged. Engines down. Cloak and Shields down. All major systems down. Warp Core critical and venting coolant plasma."
"We're done here; transfer power to the Transporters. Abandon ship!"

The fixed orbit quickly deteriorated. The Heavy Metal entered Earth's atmosphere as a massive fireball. It plunges into the Indian Ocean.

CHAPTER EIGHT
THE CALL OF DUTY

The battle in and around Afghanistan and the Arabian Sea wasn't a concise victory for either side; both sides sustained considerable losses of lives and property. Rescue teams worked around the clock to save the sailors who were in the sea; submarines, ships and helicopters from many nations worked together; commercial cruise ships were diverted to the Arabian Sea.

Sanballat boasted on the Al Jazeera Channel that he and his angels "spanked" the Aggressors, and only lost one alien ship! Terrorists throughout the world believed him, after extensive photos of the battle were broadcasted; it was hard to comprehend that one alien ship did so much damage---and Alien Kore had hundreds and even better ships---at least that's what Sanballat told the news agencies.

In every nation, memorials were held for the slain Officials and those brave men and women who lost their lives on land and sea during the Mother of All Battles. The churches held all-night prayer vigils. The ministers encouraged the people to trust God and have faith that He would make a way; that He didn't bring them this far in life to just leave them; that God delighted in the prosperity of His people.

But the battle for Earth wasn't over; the fat lady hadn't sang. Then, and only then, was the opera truly over. Gen. West had traveled across the world to spearhead the assault on Alien Kore. While others were resting, she would not. Now she met with President Kensington.

SAND HOGS

"We need to keep the pressure on Kore and Sanballat," the President said to Gen. West.
"I agree, this is far from over."
"That's an understatement. I've seen satellite photos of the Arabian Sea: It looks like a junk yard. We've got to kill or capture him; he's got weapons of mass destruction (WMD); and this isn't the Bush Administration---we know Kore stole twelve nuclear weapons!"
"Calm down sir; we're doing everything humanly possible to find Sanballat and Alien Kore."
"What the status update?"
"Sand Hogs: That's the nickname for a group of specialized construction workers who dig tunnels. I have contracted them to dig a tunnel to the Cavern."
"Now that's thought-worthy."
"Then our Special Forces Teams can get to Sanballat and Kore; we'll retrieve our gold and whatever alien technology is down there."
"I'm told by Gen. Obama of the "U.S. Space Command that there's a alien power plant down there."
"Yes, we'll take that too."
"Get down there as soon as possible. Keep me informed."

The Sandhogs were urban miners who worked underground, generally those projects involving tunneling.

The miners worked with a variety of equipment from Tunnel Boring Machines (TBM) to explosives. The Sandhogs built the foundations for most of the bridges and skyscrapers in New York City; they built the subways and sewers; built Water Tunnels #1,2,3, and the Lincoln, Holland, Queens-Midtown and Brooklyn-Battery tunnels. The tradition and honor of being a Sand Hog had been passed down from generation to generation.

CRAZY EIGHT

Throughout the world, Special Forces Teams, U.S. Marines and Navy Seals worked with the various governments to fight the spread of terrorism. The finances and network of terrorism had grown so fast that it was larger than the Gross National Product (GNP) of many Third World countries.

K-2 in Uzbekistan was back in business. The Special Forces Teams were inserted in the region. Their mission was the same: Seek and destroy Taliban, Al-Queda, Mujahideen and alien combatants.

However, hundreds of fighters were neither; they were Indian, Pakistani, Iranian, Palestinian, Saudi, Somalian, and disgruntled American But they had one thing in common: To kill Coalition Troops. But instead, many of them came there to die; Afghanistan became an elephant graveyard for those who had nothing better to do but be killed.

Sgt. Maj. Rice, 5th Special Forces, Green Berets and his men hid behind boulders that overlooked two enemy SAM sites, radar station, and at least two hundred terrorist. It was pitch black dark; there wasn't any moonlight. For a week they were on a seek-and-destroy mission to destroy overlooked missile systems, antiaircraft guns, artillery and armor vehicles. Now they had two sites, with terrorists camps within sight of each other.

The team was made up of an Intelligence Sergeant, a Weapons Sergeant, a Medical Specialist, a Demolition Sergeant, and a Communications Specialist; each man was cross-trained in another's skill area. They were accomplished by four Afghan troops that they trained.

The Berets were armed with the M-4, a version of the M-16 Assault Rifle; it was shortened, equipped with a scope, laser designation, and fired 5.56-mm 70 grain bullets with accuracy. The soldiers also had 9-mm pistols with silencers, Mark-19 Grenade Launchers, standard grenades, and C-4 explosives.

The Sgt. Maj. assembled the Special Operation Force's Laser Marker (SOFLAM). It shot out a laser beam to mark the enemy target; then laser-guided missiles could strike it.

The communications specialist called on the LST-5, the satellite radio.

> "Dark Wing, this is Crazy Eight: We have a party over here."

He electronically sent Dark Wing the coordinates.

> "We got the message: we'll bring friends."

In minutes an A-10 Thunderbolt, nicknamed "Wart Hog" came over the ridge at 400 m.p.h. When the terrorists turned the radar on, another A-10 hit it with a missile. The A-10 cost 9.8 million dollars. It was heavily protected with titanium armor; held 16,000 lbs. of bombs; had Maverick air-to-surface missiles; had a spectacular General Electric GAU-8/A Avenger 30-mm seven-barreled cannon that fired armor-piercing depleted-uranium ammunition. It could destroy any main battle tank.

The aircrafts swooped in; the maverick missiles hit their targets and destroyed the SAM systems and artillery pieces. The electric 30-mm cannons tore into the armored vehicles by firing 75 rounds per second. The special shells ripped through everything in their path. The terrorists that were left ran for rocky cover. On the second pass, the A-10s finished off whatever was still standing, or had only fallen over and was not destroyed.

The Berets stayed hidden; not knowing how many terrorists survived the attack. One sound, and they would be overrun by angry terrorists. The terrorists came out to investigate the damage and to regroup. Now the Berets saw nearly twenty of them left.

At a distance in the dark sky, was an Ac-130 Spectre Gunship. It flew only at night because it was a slow target. Its lights were out and windows darkened. It was equipped with night vision devices and thermo sensors; 4 side-mounted 105-mm cannons, 2 Bofors 40-mm cannons, and 4-25-mm Gatling Guns. When the AC-130 cut loose on the terrorists, a rain of shells and bullets fell like a sudden hail storm. It literally swept them off their feet; the area sprayed was the size of a football field. There wasn't a man standing, many were ripped to pieces.

"The party is over," the Communications Specialist told them.

"Invite us again," Dark Wing replied.

Another call came in. It was K-2, Uzbekistan, Lt. Col. John Mack.

> "Crazy Eight, this is Lucky Strike. "Sour Grapes; repeat, Sour Grapes."
>> "We got that," the Sgt. Maj. replied," let's go home."

The Berets went to the landing zone.

Several MH-47 Chinook Helicopter from Special Operations went to all the extraction points in the area. This extraction also included the Delta Force and Navy Seals Teams who were involved in the joint mission.

THE ARRIVAL

A powerful hyper-space transporter beam plowed through space. The beam entered the Earth's atmosphere and struck the ground. In a meadow stood Empress Christina Kordova, Lt. Lori Dawson and seventy-three Human Beings. These were the ones from America who elected to visit Earth; some of them would stay, and others would return at the end of the mission.

> "Isn't this like Anami to find a beautiful snowy place to reunite us with home?" Empress Christina said. "This is Columbus, Ohio, my hometown."
> "Earth," Lt. Dawson breathed in the fresh county air, "there's something about the crisp air that brings back memories."
> "Probably the gasoline fumes," Rusty said sarca-

stically, "the Centaurians used electric vehicles. Out on the ranch, we ride horses."

"Stop being cynical," Judy told him, "we're 1 lucky we didn't wind up slaves, food, or used for body parts!"

They stopped talking and stood for a moment. Some of them wept. It was so good being home; they missed their families, friends and schoolmates. Now they were grown; yet cheated out of a childhood with their parents; robbed of their innocence years by a cold universe that took more than it gave back; and cruel creatures that had no pity for others. Tears of joy mingled with wonder swept over them. The months of preparation for this moment seemed like a distant memory.

"We all have Anami Kordova and the Empire to thank for seeing us through this difficult time in our lives, Judy stated."

"That's so true. Now, from the information Lt. Dawson and I have compiled on you," Empress Christina began, "I'll transport you to your various cities. Those who plan to return with us have a communication device. Those who will stay: I love you, and have a good and prosperous life."

Christina hugged then transported them. Christina and Barbara, her personal bodyguard, transported to her Mother's last known address. Not finding her there, she went to her brother's home.

"May I help you ladies?" Carlo asked. Then he recognized Christina.

"Sis, is that you?!"

"All day long little brother."

He opened the door and hugged her. Tears of joy flooded his eyes. He hadn't cried in years; the last time was when Christina and Liliana disappeared. There wasn't a trace, not a clue what happened to them; months went by and they were presumed dead.

Carlo cried so much that month that he vowed in his heart that he wouldn't cry again---ever. So as a man, he wasn't one to show this type of emotion. But now he didn't care about some stupid teenage vow; Christina had been raised from the dead; the Death Angel released her because she wouldn't fear him.

"Where's mom?" Carlo asked.

Christina and Barbara sat in the living room with Carlo. She told Carlo the entire story from the time that Liliana and her drove down the country road to their home, until today when she and the others transported in the meadow.

"Christina, that's some story. If you had told me this five years ago, I would've thought that you were loco. But considering the recent world events, your story has great creditability. We've been invaded by galactic terrorists!"
"Yes, we're aware of what's happened; the armies of the world have been trading punches with Alien Kore."
"So your husband, Anami, came to help us fight Kore?"
"Yes, he came 17,000 light years to bring Kore to justice."
"I guess you can't get Frequent Flyer Miles, huh?"

"Not hardly; do you have any idea how far 17,000 light years is?"

"Moving along---I was never good at Math—whose your friend?"

Barbara looked Human to Carlo; her slender thighs and perky breasts made her look like a Miss America contestant.

"My name is Barbara," she said to Carlo in a realistic Human female voice. I'm an AB-E5 Artificial Intelligence being created specifically as the Empress' bodyguard."

"No way!"

"Carlo, this may be asking a lot, but I want to visit some family and friends, will you go with us?"

"Yes, if not only to see the looks on their faces; they'll be blown away. Let me get my camera."

"No camera. I'm taking a risk by even being here. My husband gave me instructions to be careful, and I always obey him."

"Tell the truth, sis..."

"I try very hard to obey him; I'm still working on it."

They left the house in Car-lo's restored 1959 Cadillac and drove to the homes of their relatives and childhood friends. All the new arrivals faced an emotional and awkward homecoming. But they brought great joy and tears of gladness in many homes, because their loved ones were back; and it was Christmas Eve.

The people of faith thanked God for answering their prayers by returning their child safely home. Their was tested in the intense fire and was proven to be genuine.

Though the abducted were now grown, in the eyes of their parents they were still children and teens. Yet, when questioned how they got back---they offered to explain later. This was a preplanned response in respect for the System Lord's mission.

It wasn't long before the F.B.I. was contacted by local law enforcement agencies that seventy-five missing children had suddenly showed up, grown up, and as healthy as Olympic athletes.

UNWANTED ATTENTION

It wasn't the victims that called the police, but the relatives who over the years formed bonds with the detectives and investigators of the Missing Persons, who ecstatically reported the return of their sons or daughters. The victims, once questioned by the authorities, gave no explanations to account for where they had been or how they returned.

Special Agents Harris and Trent from F.B.I. Headquarters, Quantico, were assigned to the case. They had a team of agents watching the new arrivals.

Harris was an average height black female. She used to be a Parole Agent, but decided to be an F.B.I. Agent. She was abusive, rude, and usually had an attitude like she was on a continuous period.

Trent was short and tough looking; he wrestled and also played center in high school. Trent graduated Harvard Law School, but decided to be an F.B.I. Agent. He was careful not to violate the Constitutional Rights of the accused. This placed him in conflict with Harris; she only wanted confessions, and didn't really care how she got them, or where the source of information came from. Occasionally she even lied in court.

Agent Atkinson of the Dept. of Homeland Security also received the information about the returning people, coined "Starbrites." His team was ordered to work with the NSA. Atkinson was 55 yrs old. He was 6ft tall; in his younger years, he was a Wall Street Stock Broker. He was a black man, very intelligent; he had bloodhound instincts when tracking fugitives. As much as he tried, he couldn't wrap his mind around what the NSA were saying about the Starbrites: That they were a high security risk people.

Agent Maxlo of the National Security Administration (NSA), and his biohazard team were ready to quarantine the Starbrites. This move was rooted in the wild assumption that the Starbrites were actually body-snatchers, alien beings who took the bodies of the Human children, then returned to invade the Earth.

Atkinson, who ran the Regional Office, was not a Science Fiction buff; he thought that Maxlo was an idiot, who was making unnecessary work for his Homeland Security Office.

CHAPTER NINE
MY BROTHER'S KEEPER

Anami Kordova was aboard the Andromeda. He looked out the window at the glorious galaxy around him. He pondered the question of why his own astronomers hadn't discovered these planets and the Human Race, but the Mutant Grays did. He wondered was there a philosophical reason; did motive play an important part in space exploration; did evil intent drive a creature harder to find ways to express itself? Was it true that evil beings only slept after they caused calamity? Or the noble slept soundly because they had done some good? And a lie was half way around the galaxy before the truth got out the room? Anyway, it was time to talk to Kore.

A hologram of Anami's image was projected to Kore. Kore was on his Moon Base and in his quarters. He was drinking out of a fifth of Crown Royal Whiskey. He was drunk.

"Kore, we need to talk."

Kore was startled. He reached for his phaser but it wasn't in his side holster, but on the dresser.

"So you're finally here, dear brother. For over a year, I've been looking over my shoulder, waiting for you to show up."
"You knew I'd come after you, so why do all those things before you left? Do you hate me and our family that much?"

"Haven't you heard---the Symbios rules my life; my will is often lost in an eddy of thousand-year-marinated evil. The Ruler lives in me through its offspring."

"Our doctors believe the Symbios can be removed. Come back and have the surgery."

"I'll die on the table."

"But if you die on the table on Centillion, at least you'll die with dignity; and everyone will know that Kore Kordova attempted to regain his true self."

"When Faye was killed, the Symbios laughed at my horror in finding her lifeless body. It was jealous of Faye; it hated her."

"So Faye was killed? I'm sorry to hear that. I heard that you two got married."

"Yes, to both of what you have said."

"Again, I sympathize with your loss; Faye was a nice female. I know that you loved her. Faye Futura will be written in the Chronicles as being a Kordova."

The liquor caused Kore to confide in his brother and expose his true feelings; this angered the Symbios. The Symbios spoke through Kore's mouth using its harsh voice.

"We don't need your sympathy. Faye was trash, irrelevant, a distraction! Kore is mine; there's nothing you can do about it!"

Kore regained control of himself.

"Now you see what I have to deal with? The Symbios has gotten stronger."

"Kore. the Humans are much like you: Strong willed. They would rather die than become your subjects. The same way you resisted the influence of the Symbios, is the way the Humans will resist you. This isn't a world ready for a System Lord like you want them to be; you want to manage the unmanageable. If you overthrow the governments of this world through terrorism, one day, in the not so distant future, today's allies be tomorrow's enemies."

"So I'm like a snake charmer charming a poisonous snake, until one day the snake bites me? Am I wrong because I want what's rightfully mine? I was born five minutes before you, and according to Centillion law, I'm the elder son, the rightful heir to the Centaurus throne. I'm the true System Lord, and you have my position."

"If you were mentally competent at the time, you would be System Lord with my blessings; as it stood, you were compromised by the Symbios, and ineligible to rule the Throne."

"How convenient for you!"

"Surrender, and I'll do everything in my power to help you."

"It's none of your business what I do. You're not my keeper; or the System Lord here. This is my star (Sun) and my planets. Go back to the Centaurus Constellation and leave me alone."

"I can't do that: You've grievously trespassed in the domains of the Synod; if I don't bring you back---two years from now they'll come to Earth in full force; and no way you'll survive. This madness must come to an end."

"As does this stupid conversation!"

Kore threw the liquor bottle at the hologram. He struggled to his feet, staggered and fell on the floor. He passed out and laid there.

Kore, Gen. Urich, Scarface and construction engineers inspected the damage to the Cavern. Repairs were made; steel girders were welded to reinforce the ceiling. Debris from the collapsed ceiling was transported atop by Transporter Plate.

"The Stargate, Shield Generator and Power Plant is fully operational," Scarface reported.

"Good, these Humans are full of surprises," Kore said, "I underestimated Kensington's resolve to use nuclear weapons. Human military history suggested that these weapons were only used as a last resort; I've pushed them too hard too soon."

"The Shield Generator diverted most of the shockwave; if it weren't for that, the Cavern would've collapsed. The impact opened several fissures."

"Right now, we have another problem: Anami is here."

"That's not good," Gen. Urich said, "how many Starships did he bring?"

"Don't know. I was drunk when he hologrammed in."

"He could have brought the entire Synod---over 800 ships?" Gen. Urich said deeply concerned.

"I doubt it; he would have said it, and I would definitely remember that; I wasn't that wasted."

CHARITY'S NOT AT HOME

Charity kissed her six year old daughter and hugged her tight. Charity was in her thirties and this was her first baby. She didn't want to leave her tonight.

> "I'll be home late, so be good and listen to the Babysitter. I love you.
> "I will mom," the child replied.

Charity drove away with a sense that everything was going to be fine, and she would be home by daybreak.

Boris Monday was leaving a New York City night club. He was the special guest of Nitty, a New York mobster. Nitty would get New York when the U.S. Military was defeated.

Monday always liked the night life, so on Earth he fitted right in. He loved the ladies and the excitement. Monday had two beautiful, sexy women, one on each side; a black and a white woman. Monday's arms were around them. He was on his way to his hotel room for a night of sexual pleasures.

Nitty was flanked by his bodyguard. Gen. Urich was close to Monday and his female friends. But atop an adjacent building a city block away was an assassin with a high-powered rifle. Crosshairs were placed upon Monday's forehead.

The assassin wore a black outfit that blended in perfectly with the roof. The assassin was a young woman of 33 years old. She was average height, brunette hair pinned up in a bun; she looked more like a librarian than a trained killer.

A flash of light was seen from atop the adjacent building, followed by a muffled sound. Boris Monday was assassinated--shot between the eyes. He crumpled to the ground and was dead.

The women screamed and ran back into the club. Nitty and his bodyguard, with weapons drawn, took cover beside a parked car.

Gen. Urich transported to the adjacent rooftop. He materialized face to face with the sniper. Both had weapons drawn.

"General, what we have here is called a Mexican Standoff."
"Who are you?"
"A single mom."
"Single mothers don't perch on rooftops and assassinate important people. I'm going to enjoy killing you; it's my serial nature."
"Enough foreplay, make a decision---shoot or boot."
"Guess I'll be on my way."
"Damn good choice. Next time we meet, the bullet is for you."
"Again, who are you?"
"Sgt. Charity, United States Marine Corp. You aliens have overstayed your welcome."

Gen. Urich transported off the roof. He had dodged a U.S.M.C. bullet; but he was humiliated because it was a woman who got the jump on him. He considered waiting a few minutes, doubling back, and catch her on her way off the roof; then decided not to because she may have a "spotter" somewhere around to assist her.

OPERATION STARBRITE

Meanwhile, Operation Starbrite was moving forward. Maxlo of the NSA and Atkinson of Homeland Security shouldered the joint responsibility. They rounded up the Starbrites, literally abducted them from their homes. The security team wore white HASMAT protective suits. They didn't knock but rammed the door off the hinges with a steel handheld battering ram. After they muscled their way in, they handcuffed the Starbrites, and hustled them into an awaiting van. They drove them to a building set up for quarantine. The Task Force didn't care what the relatives or neighbors thought, or how much the Starbrites complained about the treatment.

Miles away, Anami and Christina walked along the seashore in Miami, Florida. It was a beautiful day and the water was warm. They walked, holding hands, laughing like they were teenagers without a care in the world. Anami and Christina were so much in love. Everyone who passed them smiled and gave warm greetings.

Anami had black swimming trunks only; his chest was a little hairy. Christina wore a white two-piece bikini, and she was gorgeous. Barbara wore a pink bikini; she attracted the attention of several walkers and joggers.

They went for a swim. The water was cold but refreshing. Afterwards, they dried off and went back to the beach house they had leased. Anami and Christina had breakfast prepared by one of the cooks from the Andromeda.

"It's terrible that none of your parents are on Earth," Anami told her. "

"We knew it was a long shot. But we can discuss that later. On a much happier note, I've bought   you a white Stetson Hat: Heroes wear white hats."

"Since you bought it, I'll wear it---even to bed!"

Anami received a transmission from Captain Harmony of the Andromeda:

"Our friends are in trouble; Several Distress Signals were activated---including Lt. Lori Dawson. The U.S. Government has issued a warrant and arrested them. They have been placed in quarantine."

"Thank you Captain,"

"Honey, we must do something!" Christina cried. "Don't you go worrying about this; I'll handle the U.S. Government."

QUARANTINE

Agent Atkinson sat in his office. He looked out the plate glass window at the Starbrites in the Observation Room. The Starbrites were quarantined: Medical test such as X-rays, CAT Scans, ultrasound, DNA, blood and urine tests, and psychiatric evaluations were done on all of them; they were found to be too healthy, but Human, and with no signs of alien possession, DNA, or implants. His conclusion was that the only one possessed was Agent Maxlo; and he was possessed by the Devil.

Atkinson prided himself that he had a nose for terrorists, criminals and accomplices---and these people were neither ; they were descent, hardworking and honest.

But the polygraph examinations showed "deceptive" results. Understandable, if they were protecting someone even for a good reason.

He knew that in W.W. II, when the Nazis and Gestapo Soldiers knocked on doors asking if there were Jews in the house, many German households said "no", when in fact they hid entire families in their cellars.

One thing that he noticed was the Starbrites knew each other; a fact, since they were from different states, was next to impossible to randomly happen. The investigations revealed no prior connections between them, no pattern other than the fact they were children at the time of abduction. Another interesting thing he noticed was most of them gravitated to one person, a common denominator: He speculated that person was their leader. He pulled the file.

"Send Lori Dawson in please," Agent Atkinson requested.

Lori came into the room. She unconsciously stood at ease fashion.

"Miss Dawson, what's your rank?"
"My rank, I don't have rank?"
"You're a soldier. I can tell you're a soldier because I was once a soldier; I can tell by the way you walk, talk, stand---and how the others interact with you."
"You are incorrect with your assumption, sir."
"There you go with that "sir" stuff. Now, I'm not accusing you of being a spy, alien, or criminal of any sort; but, I need you to admit to me that you are a soldier, then I can help you."

"I have nothing to say."

"I understand: After what you've been through---abducted as a child, then abducted by us---you don't trust me, but I believe that you're on our side against Sanballat and Kore. Do you have any information for us?

"I don't know what you're talking about. May I please go?"

"Yes, you can go. I'll be here if you decide to talk."

He was disappointed. He considered threatening her and the others with incarceration at Guantanamo Bay, Cuba, but he thought that would be something Maxlo would do; and he didn't want to be like that fool.

CHAPTER TEN
GO BIG OR GO HOME!

The sleek white Jaguar pulled in front of the Greek restaurant in downtown Miami. The diver was Empress Christina. Anami and Barbara accompanied her. They exited the vehicle, and a valet parked it in the lot.

> "It's been so long since I've driven a car!" Christina exclaimed.
> "I can tell," Anami mused.
> "I'm a good driver!"
> They went in to eat lunch.

But in Miami, F.B.I. Agents Harris and Trent were closing in on Christina. They monitored Carlo, her brother's cell phone, the calls he made to Christina in Miami. Carlo's cell phone was also monitored by NSA Col. Maxlo; and using their Facial Recognition System, identified who he believed was Alien Kore, through a dozen public and secret devices hidden all over Miami; this public spying included Traffic Cams at intersections.

The NSA team met up with a Special Forces Team, Homeland Security, F.B.I, and Miami Dade Rapid Response Team. They quietly descended upon the Greek restaurant where Anami and Christina were.

Col. Maxlo, dressed in civilian clothes, went into the restaurant. At a corner table, he saw Barbara and Christina. Next to Christina, he saw who he believed was

Alien Kore. Maxlo casually walked out the door.

"Christina and Kore are in there. There's also another woman, probably an alien; the women are considered, collateral but Alien Kore must not escape!"

"So, we're just going to kill them because they're eating lunch with Alien Kore?" Atkinson asked dryly, fed up with Maxlo's Neanderthal ways.

"Agent, let me do my job. You don't know what resources these aliens have. Any moment a space-craft could appear and disintegrate this whole damn block and us with it."

In the restaurant, Christina spilled red wine on her beautiful sun dress.

"Oh, I need to go to the ladies' room."
"Go ahead, dear, hurry back."

She left with Barbara.

The Task Force came through the front and side doors. One of the men tripped over another's foot; his weapon discharged. All the troops started shooting. The patrons ducked and threw themselves, wives and children under the tables. Two waiters got shot; several patrons were injured by shattered plates, glasses and wood fragments from the tables, posts and hardwood floors. The troops, used fully automatic M-4 Assault Rifles, and saturated the entire corner where Anami was with zinging lead.

But the System Lord already suited-up with his shiny black armor; the bullets disintegrated on contact with his force shield.

The crystal jewel embedded in his headset emanated red and white alternating energy fields; it was Anami's choice which weapon to use. He levitated off the ground a couple of feet. White light erupted from the crystal. A wave of energy enveloped the room. The sudden pressure, blew all the windows out of the restaurant; the liquor bottles, glasses and mirrors on the walls shattered. The wave swept the soldiers off their feet; some of them were completely thrown out the shattered windows onto the sidewalk.

Their assault rifles and pistols crumbled in their hands; the molecular structure that made them real to the touch was interrupted and the weapons fell apart and disintegrated. Even the mental energy, the natural force in the men was temporarily depleted and they fell unconscious but still alive.

At the sound of gunfire, Barbara threw herself against the back wall of the bathroom. The wall was cinder block, but she broke through it easily. She knew the System Lord was being attacked; she also knew he could take care of himself; but Christina wasn't impervious to bullets, or had a force shield.

"Follow me," Barbara said.
"I left the transport unit in the hotel room," she said.

Both Christina and Barbara wore four-inch heels. Normally they could walk but not run in them.

"Take off the heels," Barbara said, "We have to move fast."

They left the heels in the bathroom, and went through

the hole in the wall. Barbara took Christina's hand. They ran down the alley. But stopped at the corner.

"Hands in the air!" The Miami Dade Officers demanded.
Christina and Barbara complied.
"Better let me handle this," Barbara whispered.

Barbara was quick. She grabbed the assault rifles from two Officers and snapped them like rotten twigs. The third officer fired his weapon but her hand stopped the bullet two inches from the barrel; she took the rifle and whacked him over the head with it.

"Run Christina!" She yelled as she kept the Officers busy.

Barbara advanced and beat the Officers mercilessly. They hit her with over 100 rounds but she kept coming. She beat them down with her bare fists. An armor vehicle tried to run her over but she moved out the way, went around the side, picked it up and turned it over.

I front of the restaurant the System Lord battled the remaining members of the Assault Team. The wounded and unconscious were dragged to safety, the patrons in the restaurant exited through the back and side doors. The Team fired .50 caliber bullets from the mounts of armored vehicles, but Anami keep coming at them They hit him with a LAW missile but to no avail. Suddenly, Anami raised his hands in a pushing motion; he pushed the Assault Team vehicles, parked cars and men fifty yards down the street. None of them dared to come back after him.

Christina ran as fast as she could. After a while she got

Tired and started walking.

People looked at her beautiful sun dress and wondered why she didn't have any shoes. Then a black car stopped beside her.

"You can't run forever," Agent Trent said.

Trent and Harris got out the car.

"Christina," Harris said dryly.

Harris searched Christina for weapons, handcuffed, and put her in the back seat of the car. They headed for F.B.I. Headquarters.

"You're either a terrorist or sympathizer," Harris said. "You're responsible for the death of my son."
"That's not true and you know it," Christina snapped.
"Kore and the other woman are dead."
"And the Moon is made of cheese."
"Oh, you think this is funny?"
"No, I just don't believe you're telling the truth."
"Then, believe this: You'll rot in Federal Prison for a hundred years. And since you're an American, if convicted of treason during a state of war, you'll get the needle!"
"Lighten up, Harris," Trent told her," save your interrogation for the video tape!"

They arrived at the F.B.I. Headquarters in Miami. Once inside, they put her in an Interrogation Room. Harris placed one of Christina's wrist in the handcuff attached to the desk. Harris was in her element. But Trent frowned. He'd had enough of Agent Harris' shock tactics.

"What's your full name?" Harris asked.
"You already know that."
"Where were you born?"
"You know that too."

Harris got angry. She slapped Christina across the mouth. Christina wiped a drop of blood from her lip. She knew without a doubt she could whip this woman.

"You'll answer my questions!"
"You'll pay for this bitch!" Christina mumbled.

With her unchained hand, Christina slapped Harris. Harris was shocked. No one ever hit her back; she was the F.B.I. She drew back to strike her again.

Trent grabbed Harris' raised arm. He pulled her away from Christina. Harris had struck another suspect; he wish he could unchain Christina's hand so she could teach Harris a lesson.

Col. Maxlo and Agent Atkinson arrived. They hadn't seen what transpired.

"Christina is our prisoner." Maxlo stated. "There will be no more questions, no photos, video tape, finger-prints or file kept on her. And, by the way, we were never here."

Col. Maxlo and Atkinson took Christina away.

Five miles away at the Greek Restaurant, Anami, still wearing the black SLW (System Lord Weapon) looked for Christina. He checked the women's bathroom. He saw the hole in the wall; that the concrete blocks were all outside, thus no one broke in but out.

Inside not outside the bathroom, showing that they broke out and no one broke in. Barbara came back through the hole in the wall. Her clothes were ragged with bullet holes; she was dirty, but functioning within the specified manufactures' perimeters.

> "Christina didn't have her transporter unit, so I made an escape route. But the Police were waiting outside. I told Christina to run while I delayed the Police."
>
> "So she's out there somewhere," Anami said. "but she's on her home planet; we'll find her. You did a good job."

They transported back to the Andromeda.

PEACE WITH HONOR

"How did this happen," General?"

"At first I thought Nitty set us up; then I discovered it was a Government-sanctioned assassination. A whole squad was there. I barely got away."

He wouldn't tell Kore that a single mom stared him down and forced him to leave the rooftop.

> "Monday brought a lot of finances into the League; he'll be hard to replace."
>
> "Kore, you have a message from the Pentagon."

Kore patched in with his implant. This was also how he communicated with the Cavern and Moon Base

"This is General West, Chairwoman of the Joint Chiefs of Staff. The President is weary of the conflict with the League, he seeks a peaceful resolution. The phrase he wants to use is: "Peace With Honor." So to demonstrate his good faith in the Truce, he'll return your wife, Christina as soon as possible."

"I'll get back to you," Kore replied.

Kore told the other what had transpired.

"Outstanding!" Scarface exclaimed.

"It's uncanny," Gen. Urich added.

"They killed my wife, and think Christina is her. Yes, I'll use her as leverage to stop Anami."

"When Anami discovers what the Pentagon has done, he'll join us against the Americans," Scarface added.

The three Starships remained parked in space near Planet Saturn, out of Kore's range. Scanners on the vessels were so powerful and accurate, they still monitor Earth. Anami wasn't his usual vibrant self after returning from Earth without Christine. He felt that a part of him was ripped off and discarded. He felt miserable, but didn't want his crew to know it; but losing Christine was like the Sun gone down on him.

"We intercepted a message from the Pentagon to Kore. There will be an exchange today: Christina for peace," Captain Harmony said." They believe Christina is Kore's wife."

"They obviously don't know what she looks like; all they know is what Kore looks like."

"The nerve of Kore using Christina as bate," Captain Harmony said. "He has no shame!"

"It is what it is---as the Humans say," Anami replied, then transported off the Bridge.

President Kensington was in a secret bunker with Gen. West. It was the Morning Briefing. Information came to him in a continuous stream. The tension in the world was increasing. The leaders of the nations were nervous as they waited impatiently for the next alien attack.

He sanctioned Operation Starbrite as a precaution. He also sanctioned the botched attempt to eliminate Kore at the Greek Restaurant; he watched it as it happened on live video feed. He was not proud the way Col. Maxlo handled it, the civilian causalities and all. However, the detainment of Kore's wife in exchange for peace seemed promising.

But in the back of his mind, things didn't compute; he was confused why Kore in the Body Armor didn't kill any of the Task Force. They hit him with everything immediately available, but Kore purposely avoided killing anyone; even the survivors fighting the android, claimed that she could have easily killed them but didn't.

He reached into his briefcase. This case was called "The Football." It contained nuclear launching codes. A nuclear weapon couldn't be launched by America without the President of the United States giving the authorization code. Only two presidents had to make that decision: Kensington did when the B-2 Spirits attacked the Heavy Metal above the Arabian Sea. The spacecraft had nearly destroyed the U.S., NATO, Russian and Chinese Navies. This time Kensington wasn't looking for the Nuclear Launch Codes, but the Red Phone.

The President and Gen. West disappear. They reappeared in a Conference Room aboard the Andromeda as it orbited Saturn. Saturn was seen through the large glass windows. They also saw the other two Starships, with guns big enough to knock the Moon out of orbit.

Anami stood before them in his System Lord Uniform but wearing the white Stetson hat Christina bought him.

President Kensington was almost speechless. As a politician, this was the first time in his career that he struggled for words. It may have been he was holding back the tears, as he thought of being tortured to death.

"The end of the road, Pres. Kensington sighed.

Anami wanted to laugh but it would have been undiplomatic and take away his serious demeanor.

"Not quite. Mr. President, and General West. I'm Anami Kordova, the System Lord of the Centaurus Constellation, also known as the Empire..

"Is "Kordova" short for Alien Kore?" President Kensington asked in apprehension.

"Ah---no; I'm his twin brother."

"Whew! My heart almost stopped."

"I waited to hear the "Resistance is Futile" line." Gen. West Added.

"I used that line when I asked Empress Christina to marry me."

"Christina is your wife? Pres. Kensington blurted.

"Yes, and it was me having a quiet lunch in the Greek Restaurant, when I was most rudely interrupted by hot lead; so release her to me."

"Of course, Immediately."

"Thank you. I came here to arrest Kore for crimes done in my jurisdiction."

"Are you some type of Super Hero? I saw the black suit and the energy ray," Gen. West asked.

"I don't know how to answer that, since I don't know what qualifies one as a Super Hero. Take a look out the window; we have 200 hundred of these and thousands of smaller spacecrafts; so we depend on technology more than "super powers.""

"What can we do to help?" Pres. Kensington inquired.

"Right now, there's the matter of the people you call Starbrites. They are human beings who years ago were abducted by rogue scientists, the Mutant Grays. We rescued them off a slave ship; but not knowing where to return them, brought them home with us; we took good care of them; they have lived with us as citizens in good standing. Many of the Starbrites were here visiting relatives and desire to return to Centaurus. My request is that you release them, and treat the ones who stay on Earth with dignity."

"That request is granted: No one left behind," Pres Grant responded. "By the way, nice hat."

"Thank you; Christina picked it out. Tell the world leaders that the true Centaurians are peacemakers and peacekeepers. After this is over, we'll open diplomatic talks."

The president and general were transported back to the Bunker. President Kensington kept his word and made the call. Two hours later, Empress Christina and the Starbrites were released from custody.

Aboard the Andromeda, when Christina saw Anami, she ran to him and wrapped her legs around his waist. She kissed him passionately on the lips. The Bridge crew was present and applauded.

"My dear, we're in public," Anami said, though he enjoyed it. She was totally ecstatic.

He missed her, but couldn't let anyone know that it was tearing him apart while she was gone. The days were long and the nights were lonely. In his mind, he pictured her being abused by sadistic interrogators, or locked in a cold, lonely cell without food, water, or anyone to talk too. He'd heard the American Military and the C.I.A often used torture to get information from suspected terrorists and he hoped she wasn't Waterboarded.

The Bridge crew took turns hugging Christina. They were happy that she was alive and well. Things could've gone very wrong with all the guns blazing in the restaurant; it could have been another unnecessary Faye Futura tragedy.

"I'm glad you're safe," Barbara said.

TUNNEL VISION

It was sunrise over the Hindu Kush Mountains as the Special Operations MA-47 Chinook Helicopter, for Special Operations, touched down at K-2. Dark Wing was a joint C.I.A. and Special Forces post in Uzbekistan. Airstrikes and Drone attacks initiate from here. In the helicopter were the Sandhogs, the skillful and mighty tunnel-drilling team. Also aboard were Special Operations Gen. Obama, Sgt. Maj. Rice, Major Mills of the U.S. Army Corp of Engineers, and Lt. Dawson.

Sgt. Major Rice was a rugged man. He's 35 years old, bald, 6-2 and athletic build. He had big arms and legs like tree trunks. Luka was Polish, a 45-year-old rugged construction expert with a thick New York accent. He was the civilian Superintendant of Construction for the 32-man Sandhogs drilling team. They were escorted to the Briefing Room. In the room was the Special Forces Team and bags of weapons, ammunition, explosives and other necessities to wage war in the Cavern.

"Welcome to K-2. It's a great day to destroy the works of the devil!" Gen. Obama stated.

"The General hates terrorists," Sgt. Maj. Rice explained, hunting them down and bringing them to justice is his ministry."

"We've found a cave," Maj. Mills began: "The assignment is to tunnel diagonally 2 miles from the cave until reaching the Cavern."

"Then Special Forces backed up by Lt. Dawson of the Centaurus Empire will storm the Cavern," Sgt. Major Rice told them.

"What's the Centaurus Empire?" Luka asked.

"It's a long story," Gen. Obama told him, "but Lt. Dawson is cleared by Pres. Kensington.

"You're under the protection of America's best," Sgt. Major Rice stated. "We'll be near you at all times. For your protection, you cannot leave the cave for any reason unless authorized by me. Your machinery and equipment is already at the cave and assembled. We have extra laborers available if you need them."

"Thank you Sgt. Major," Col. Mack said. "As you tunnel, at times you'll hear distant explosions. We'll continue military operations in the vicinity to cover up the sound of the tunnel machines. But we won't call in airstrikes while you're underground."

"That's comforting," Luka said dryly.

"That's it; time to rock and roll!" Gen. Obama announced.

"I thought he was going to say, "can you dig it," Luka whispered to Lt. Dawson. "Then I would respond, "of course I can---I'm a Sandhog."

"Don't make fun of my hero," Lt. Dawson replied with a smile.

"I want to hear that long story you have to tell."

"Get us to the Cavern and the exclusive is all yours---including a steak dinner, if you're not predisposed."

"I'll clear my schedule."

The chosen cave was well hidden. It was located 2.5 miles north of the Cavern. It was a large cave. The Sandhogs found the equipment ready to go, because the Army Corp of Engineers were professionals. The assignment: Bore diagonally 2.5 miles from the back of the cave at a specific decline as guided by GPS until reaching the Cavern.

As operations continued throughout the day and night, side rooms were constructed to store the second TBM, explosives, equipment, living quarters and a command center. The Green Berets and Navy Seals also had their own rooms to prepare for the assault on the Cavern.

Electricity to power the equipment was generated by an alien device supplied by the Empire; all the equipment used was electrical in nature, as not to make excessive noise.

The Sandhog team consisted of enough men for three

continuous shifts. Luka and his assistant, Leonard supervised the crew of 3 TBM operators, 3 mechanics, 3 shuttle drivers, 3 Bobcat loader drivers, 2 explosive experts, and 10 construction workers. Working outside the cave were 3 Caterpillar Loader operators, and 3 giant earth-moving truck drivers.

Hours the TBM clawed through the rock. The diamond-tipped cutters shaped the tunnel as it went. The machinery used was either electric/ battery powered. The rock and dirt was loaded by the Bobcat into the shuttle debris bins; the shuttle driver drove the debris outside and dumped it; then the Caterpillar Loader operator loaded the debris into the earthmover trucks; and the truck driver drove it to a nearby cliff and dumped it.

This operation was different than tunneling under New York City: There were no terrorists bent on killing them on sight, or at the other end of the tunnel. Therefore, they had to be quiet.

The tunnel was 12ft. wide and 8ft. tall. It was reinforced every hundred feet by a welded steel frame. Ventilation, electrical conduits and ceiling lights were installed as the TBM moved ahead. The purpose of the tunnel wasn't to drive vehicles through, a two-lane highway, but to get to the Cavern as fast as possible, and provide reasonable access for the strike team.

DELTA QUADRANT

Meanwhile, millions of miles away, P-209 was a planet used as a nursery for Symbios. It was surrounded by swamp and dense jungle. Here the Throxs, galactic mercenaries, who worked or fought for anyone who paid them, supervised and guarded the Symbios Pool for the Ruler of Chud. They walked the perimeter with saber tooth tiger beasts.

2000 Human Beings from Planet Earth, youth thru senior citizens worked feverishly throughout the massive compound. Thousands of Humans had arrived, worked their entire lives, and died of old age while tending the Symbios. It was either work or be sold again: Dismembered for body parts, as meat, or the Scientific Laboratory of Dr. Q. Human trafficking from Earth had been going on for untold centuries.

Liliana Santiago looked up at the hot alien sun and wiped the sweat from her face. She and Sherry Dawson were prisoners forced as caretakers of the Symbios Pool that belongs to the Ruler, the System Lord of Chud.

> "I'm tired of this place and all this work," Liliana complained.
> "We have to keep going," Sherry encouraged.
> "I dreamt about my Christina last night,"
> "I always see Lori——all grown up and wearing the Miss America crown. I'm sure her red hair is like fire right now."

The Throxs Leader, a 7-foot reptile creature, headed towards them. He saw Sherry and Liliana talking.

> "I told you two what would happen if you kept talking! Stop talking and work more!" He bellowed with a snarl. "The Symbios are still hungry----do you want to be their next meal?"

The Throx Leader prodded Liliana and Sherry with a

with a metal rod. Green energy came out their eyes and mouth. They screamed in pain.

Mu Galaxy Cruiser

Aboard the Andromeda: Capt. Harmony moved closer to Earth; the other Starships followed. She paused to acknowledge an alarm signal on her console.

> "Long-range sensors detect the reactor signature of a Mu Galaxy Cruiser."
> "Hyper Jump," Anami ordered.
> "Attention crew: Battle Stations. We're going in hot!" Captain Harmony ordered.

An alarm sounds and the crew rushed to their stations. Interceptor Pilots put on their flight suits and climbed into their VXT Interceptors. These Interceptors had white Empire Crescent on both sides of their cockpits.

Turret Gunners occupied the consoles on the Battle Bridge, a raised section of the Main Bridge. Crewmembers operated the Phaser Gatling Guns. The Missile Room Crew loaded and armed the missiles.

Camouflaged with cloak technology, from deep craters on the Earth side of the Moon, hydraulic platforms emerged. On the platforms were anti-spacecraft Gatling Guns, Proton and Nuclear Missiles on modified SAM launchers.

Aboard the Mu Galaxy Cruiser, Gen. Urich and Scarface watched the view screen as Andromeda and the other ships came into firing range. He also saw the Empire Interceptors racing towards the Moon.

"Fire!" Gen Urich ordered.

Missiles launched; the phaser Gat-lings fired thousands of rounds at the Empire Interceptors, but were unable to stop them. Two American Made Nuclear Missiles struck the rotating shields of Andromeda. They exploded with ultra bright flashes.

> "Damage report," Anami asked.
> "No damage or causalities."
> "Good. Fire Main Batteries."

Energy beams from the Andromeda bombarded the weapon platforms and destroyed them. The ordinance elevators exploded with secondary explosions that sent Humans, aliens and machinery drifting into orbit.

It was night time in the U.S. The citizens of Earth stood in their yards, in the streets, some watched on television, as the spectacular battle waged on and near the Moon. Then the Mu Galaxy-Class Cruiser came around the eastern hemisphere of the Moon to confront the Andromeda.

> "They're powering up weapons," Captain Harmony warned.
> "Kore, this is your last chance," Anami warned him in his most serious tone.
> "Kore isn't here; and we're not going back to prison!" Gen. Urich replied.
> "He's going to make a Hyper Space Jump," Captain Harmony advised.
> "Take him out!"

Four Quadrex Missiles zipped out the launchers and destroyed the Mu Galaxy Cruiser. Gen. Urich, Scarface, and everyone aboard were killed.

On the back side of the Moon, twenty VXT Interceptors, with the League Emblem, came up from an underground airstrip beneath the dome. This was their ace-in-the-hole, a sneak attack---each ship rigged to explode on contact with multiple nuclear warheads.

The Andromeda fired a special missile. It went through the dome of the Moon Base. It penetrates deep underground. The entire base imploded, was sucked into the depths of the Moon and disintegrated. Kore's Interceptors never launched.

> "You didn't need me" Commander Hur radioed.
> "Wisdom of war is always bring more firepower than needed."

The Sandhogs arrived at the Cavern wall. The TBM machines were put away and the civilians exited the tunnel. A Demolition Expert attached C-4 Shape Charge Explosives on the wall.

> "Fire in the hole!" He yelled.

The C-4 explosive blasted a large opening in the wall.

Sgt. Maj. Rice and his team, Lt. Dawson and her team stormed into the Cavern. Gunfire erupted. The fighting became furious, the casualties on both sides mounted. Industrial machinery occupied a lot of space, so there were ample places to hide behind.

Automatic phaser weapons mounted on the walls fire upon the Teams. robotic platform with active weapons glided down the center of the floor towards Lt. Dawson. It was difficult for her to advance. But the Centaurians used their energy grenade launchers. They destroyed the automated weapons and robotic platform without bring the ceiling down on top of themselves.

More Special Forces soldiers arrived. They came in like a pack of starving wolves. Lt. Dawson and Sgt. Maj. Rice fought their way to the Control Room. Lt. Dawson found the Shield Generator and shut it off.

In the Stargate Room, Kore, Dr. Q and the Mutant Gray Assistants prepared to abandon the Cavern. Sanballat was also with them.

> "Take me with you!" Sanballat begged.
> "You're Human and no use to me."

Kore pulled out his phaser. Sanballat ran out the room.

Kore went to the console. He typed the Stargate Address to P-109. Kore activated the Stargate. Kore, Dr. Q and the Mutant Gray Assistants left the Cavern.

With the Shield Generator down, the System Lord transported into the midst of the battle; he was in his SLW suit. This time the energy beam coming from his helmet was red and lethal.

He became a killing machine. He levitated above the floor; then out of compartments on his wrist, white dart-like spears ejected. These spears penetrates through the metal machinery and even the stone walls, and killed the combatants. He was the type of soldier that Earth Generals only dreamed of. The rest of the combatants quickly surrendered when they realized they were dealing with alien technology.

Anami, Gen. West and several troops meet up with Lt. Dawson and Sgt. Major Rice in the Stargate Room.

The SLW reclined and Anami read the Stargate Console. Soldiers came to the door with startling discoveries.

"Look who we found!"

They had Sanballat in handcuffs. But they also found the hostages: Vice-President Reed, Pres. Bogotto, Pres. Soto, and Comdr. Gen. Perry.

"We owe our lives to Faye Futura," Vice-Pres. Reed said. "She pleaded with Kore not to kill us--- and he loved her so much he honored her request. Instead of killing us, he transported us to a room."
"This is his brother, Anami Kordova," Lt. Dawson told them.
"There's a glass case with a female body in it," a soldier reported.
"It's Faye, she was killed a while back," Vice-Pres. Reed said. "I thought Kore would kill us after that, but he just stopped talking to us."

"We'll take Faye with us. She's a Kordova and will be laid to rest as such," Anami told them. "I believe that if it weren't for her in his life, Kore would have done more harm."

Anami studied the computer consol further.

"Kore went to P-109. It's a tropical planet the System Lord of Chud reigns over."
"Let's go after him," Gen. West eagerly suggested.
"Want some off-world action, huh?" Anami responded. "Your time has definitely come."

"Always wanted to be an Astronaut---just couldn't stay clear from the donut shop!"

Anami dialed the Stargate. It activated; he suited up again and the Team, minus the politicians, passed through the Gate. The Strike Team materialized at P-109, where the Symbios Spanning Pool and Human slave labor camp was. Kore and his associates weren't in sight. Seeing the System Lord, the Throxs trampled madly through the jungle to get away..

Liliana, Sherry, and others emerged from behind the Symbios tanks. Lt. Dawson sees Sherry, her mother.

> "Mom!" She cried out.
> "It's me. And this is my friend, Liliana," Sherry tells her.
> "Christina will be thrilled to see you," Anami told her.
> "How is Christina---do you know her well?"
> "Yes, very well," Anami said with a smile.

The Humans were evacuated through the Stargate. The Empire and Special Forces Team searched for Kore and his loyal followers. Kore and the others couldn't be found.

In New York City, the Sandhogs received a tickertape hero's welcome. The News Agencies carried the story of how the Sandhogs, working around the clock, tunneled to the Cavern, and gave the military access to Alien Kore's Headquarters; which also lead to the rescue of the Politicians, and 2,000 off-world Human slaves.

Sanballat, the Earth Marshall was tried by the International Tribunal; he was found guilty of Crimes Against Humanity, and hanged by the neck until he was dead. F.B.I. Agent Harris was forced to resign due to her mental breakdowns. And Col. Maxwell was demoted because of the way he endangered civilian lives, including women and children in Miami.

A delegation from Earth enjoyed a dinner party aboard the Andromeda. This included Pres. Kensington, Gen. West, Lt. Dawson, Liliana, Sherry, the Starbrites and parents, plus foreign dignitaries. The major news agencies were also invited. Luka and the Sandhogs were also present.

> "A toast to our new friends," Anami began, " and the reunion of families; and to those who kept Hope alive!"
> "Amen to that!" Christina agreed.

CHAPTER ELEVEN
ULEMEN

P-222 Ulemen was located in the Delta Quadrant. It was a tropical paradise twelve Light Years from the Home World of the Grand Exalted Ruler of Chud, a ruthless predatory System Lord.

On this sunny day birds sang in the jungle trees. Small animals leaped from limb to limb, curious but nonetheless unafraid of the people below.

The Ulemens were a humble people, a primitive civilization of humanoids. They sailed the sea and explored the vastness of their mostly uncharted world. Cameron was the name of their modest village. An avenue ran through the village and divided it into halves. On both sides of the street the houses were woven with thatched roofs. There was no electronic technology anywhere on the planet.

The women and children gathered fruits and vegetables from the jungle's inexhaustible supply, while the older males casted their nets into the tranquil sea and reaped the abundance of fish and assorted seafood.

Chief Rama stood on the shore and marveled at the ships. He was extremely old. His lanky body of 500 years remained strong though wrinkled with age. He was six-foot-five and weighed only two hundred pounds. He had deep green eyes.

"What a magnificently beautiful day, Ulemen Chief Rama said to Xandi, his lovely wife.
"It was made especially for you," she replied.
"Thank you dear, so sweet of you to say that. Look: The sea is alluring, so peaceful; the fishing vessels are full. They ride low in the water. I can't wait to see what they have caught!"
"I know you miss the sea. But you had more than your share of adventures---over 400 years."

He nodded in agreement. They strolled along the edge of Cameron. Chief Rama was bronze, tall and arrow thin and Xandi was the same. Her hair, like peppered silk, flowed down her back to her waist.

The couple paused momentarily their stroll to further examine the ships that came to shore; these ships were artistically painted; some looked like dragons or mystical sea monsters conjured by the imaginations of their spirited owners.

He kisses his beautiful wife. She responds with a strong embrace. The villagers pretend like they don't' see them, though they knew they were so in love with life, their people and their personal relationship.

The jungle erupted in panic. Animals raced in every direction. Lightning rent the clouds. Eerie fog rolled in from the sea onto the land. The sky became charcoal black. Hail the size of walnuts pounded the village and surrounding jungle. Then heavy snow mixed with freezing rain glazed over everything.

The primitive Ulemens were afraid; they had never witnessed such a drastic climate change. Fear of death and destruction clutched their hearts.

Out of the sky descended a massive black spacecraft with silver talons etched into its hull: The symbol of an evil dynasty, the Ruler of Chud.

The Ulemens were spellbound because they had never seen a spaceship; this was arrival of the Starship Silver Hawk. It hovered above the village.

Chief Rama and Xandi froze in terror at the hateful creature that watches them; there was a menace in its stare, an oppression, an unfathomable wickedness.

The Ruler of Chud breathed and made a wheezing suction sound. The creature came directly toward them.

The Ruler was a large creature with hairy octopus-type multi-legs and clawed feet; it wore the most fitful black garment and was hooded. Only its red eyes were seen like fiery orbs projected off of a charcoal face; its many arms were huge and muscular. Each hand has a single silver claw that was six inches long and razor sharp. In one of its forward hands was an ivory staff with a pulsating red jewel attached.

> "I am the Grand Exalted Ruler of Chud. I am your god and you will serve me!"
> "I will do no such thing," Chief Rama calmly responded."
> "Foolish creature, maybe this will convince you!"

The GER tapped his staff on the ground: A beam of red light lassoed Chief Rama around his neck. It picked him off the ground. His feet kicked wildly because he was choking to death.

"Put him down!" Xandi demanded, yet her feeble words fell on uncaring ears.

The GER waited until Chief Rama almost passed out, then sits him down.

"I am your god, the object of your worship. You will never talk to me like that again. Do you understand me?"

Holding his throat, Chief Rama nodded in compliance.

"A wise decision. I annex your world as part of my Domain. Your people and others will care for my Symbios. You will be rewarded for obedience, and punished for disobedience. You'll live according to my will, or die because of it. I will leave for now but my servants shall remain. There's nothing further to discuss!"

The Ruler of Chud transported back onto his ship. A large cargo door opened and Kore, Dr. Q and a regiment of Throxs marched five hundred Human slaves down the long ramp to the planet surface.

"My destiny is to become a System Lord, not a Symbios babysitter" Kore tells Dr. Q.
"Be patient, this is only temporary. The Ruler has much bolder plans for you."
"I know: The Earth Coalition thinks they've seen the last of me. They have no idea who they're dealing with, nor my persistence and resources. I'll humble and defeat them, or bombt them back to the Stone Age."

Hours of backbreaking work immediately commenced once the Throx Cargo Freighters arrived bringing Symbios Pools, equipment and thousands of Symbios. Throx Cruisers and Troops also arrived.

THE EARTH TERRITORIAL FLEET

After the decisive victory over the forces of Alien Kore, negotiations between the Centaurians and the Human Race were successful. The majority in the Synod of System Lords who ruled various territories welcomed the citizens of the new Designation: P-225-Planet Earth as friends and allies; but others watched with a cautious and watchful eye.

Nevertheless, political, business, commerce and technological agreements were signed including a 20-year joint space exploration venture.

General West sat at her desk. It had been five years since she left the Pentagon as the first female Chairwoman of the Joint Chiefs of Staff. Now she was the Commanding General of the Earth Territorial Fleet (ETF) in compliance with the Joint Exploration Agreement (JEA) with the Centaurians.

This was her dream job. She had always wanted to be an Astronaut but never applied at NASA. She always thought that she wasn't Astronaut material, but could serve America in a different capacity.

Her outstanding military record brought recognition and promotions: Brig. Gen., LT. Gen., Maj. Gen., and then General. Her Pentagon duty brought her to the attention of President Kensington. She was chosen as Chairwoman of the Joint Chiefs of Staff.

Then when Alien Kore attacked, she stepped up to the plate and destroyed the Heavy Metal. When Anami Kordova, the System Lord arrived on Earth and she took her first off-world adventure, she was hooked on visiting alien worlds and civilizations; Earth's land, sea and air wasn't good enough anymore. Then she knew for certain her destiny was ultimately linked to space travel.

She traveled to the Centaurus Empire and for two years trained with their Special Unit on Planet Centillion. She wouldn't trade that for anything.

The Headquarters of the Earth Territorial Fleet was the New Mexico desert site of the former Top Secret base called Area 51. The base was vastly reconstructed with superstructures, runways, large hangers and a mile-deep subterranean Army Base with a Stargate.

Above ground were facilities to build Starships and the new ETF Interceptors, weapons and space vehicles.

The Starships Constitution, Eisenhower and Coral Sea were built as the results of the Joint Exploration Agreement with the Centaurians. They were outfitted with the latest alien and Earth technologies, integrated to make the applications user friendly for a quick study by the already well-trained combat pilots. The onboard computers did the science and navigation, though there were scientists and engineers aboard from both worlds.

In the subterranean control room where the Stargate was located, a siren blared: The Stargate activated. The large video screen came alive. Anami Kordova, Christina, their two year old son, Jason, and now Lt. Comdr. Lori Dawson came through the Stargate.

"Greetings from Centillion," Anami said, "peace and prosperity to our friends and allies on Earth."

"Sounds good so far," Gen. West replied. "I see you made this visit a family affair."

"Not exactly," Anami responded. "There has arisen an urgent situation that you may be interested in resolving. It also may also be the most dangerous mission yet."

"Count me in."

"Wait to you hear what it is. First of all, we sent a Recon Drone into the Domain of the Grand Exalted Ruler of Chud."

"No you didn't," West laughed.

"Yes we did. Now, keep in mind we don't as a matter of policy start conflicts, interfere or convert other civilizations to think or act like us, but our National Security Directive compels us to watch our enemies, those who demonstrate hostility towards the Empire or our friends.

"So, what evil has he done lately?" Gen. West seriously asked.

"We have evidence that P-222 Ulemen was recently conquered by The Ruler of Chud. Our Drone's life-form-sensors also detected and photographed Human Beings on Ulemen."

"More Human slaves out there?"

"Yes, approximately 500."

"We believe Dr. Q. abducted them from Earth and sold them to the Ruler of Chud," Lt. Comdr. Dawson added.

"I can't sleep at night knowing there are people from Earth out trapped out there without hope of ever getting back to Earth," Christina confided, " I can imagine how they feel; my mother told me about the suffering and misery! I can imagine how I'd feel if some took Jason away from me."

"Do you have a rescue plan?" Gen. West asked. "Something of this magnitude, I'll have to clear with the President If we're not careful, this can very easily lead to war with the GER."

"We'll be successful without causing a war. However, Empire and Synod Vessels are known to the GER's Throx Security Troopers. I purpose that Earth ships be used."

"Tell me more about the Grand Exalted Ruler so I can brief the President," Gen. West asked.

"The GER is an asexual creature," Anami told her, "and the last "breeder" of her kind: The others died two thousand years ago from a plague that was said to had been released on the planet by an enemy. This lone creature survived because it was genetically different from the others--- and basically a Mutant."

"I have enough to present to the President and ETF officials."

"After President Kensington gives you the Green Light to proceed, I will present the plan to the Synod. The commonality and joint effort being that Humans are enslaved. I'm sure the Synod will agree to our mutual interest in this matter."

In two hours Gen. West had orders from the President: Liberate the Humans on 222-Ulemen. The coordinates of Ulemen were sent to Gen. West; twelve hours later the Starship Coral Sea, Capt. John Mack and Special Forces Team SF-1 led the voyage from Earth to the other rim of the Milky Way Galaxy. Two other Earth ships the Starship Constitution and Eisenhower were also diverted to the rescue mission.

The SF-1 Team consisted of recently promoted Capt. John Mack as the Captain of the Starship Coral Sea. Under him were Maj. Melvin Rice, Maj. Effie Hall, Lt. Eric Chavez and Professor Ryan Shariyat.

Capt. Mack was a Lt. Colonel formally deployed at K-2 Uzbekistan. He fought gallantly against the local terrorists groups led by Alien Kore and Sanballat. He was a career soldier who volunteered for off-world reassignments. Mack was known for his hatred of terrorists. He was granted this assignment because he was a fearless patriot who was not afraid to make tough decisions.

Sgt. Effie Hall served under Gen. West in the Pentagon. Hall coordinated operations in Afghanistan against the locals, Kore and Sanballat. She also worked with Lt. Comdr. Lori Dawson and the Centaurians.

Hall was the top self-defense instructor at Ft. Bragg. She trained the Green Beret candidates in hand-to-hand combat. She was a 40-year old black woman, athletic, agile, and at times brazen. Her Pentagon Code Name was "Perfect Storm."

Lt. Eric Chavez was a recent graduate from the Green Beret program. This was his first deployment. He was 25 years old, an orphan bounced around several foster homes; he was dubbed an incorrigible child. After four years of college he became bored and dropped out. Then he discovered a profession that interested him and something he was good at: Killing people, a Sniper.

Pro. Ryan Shariyat was 17 years old when he started working for the U.S. Army. He was a genius who graduated from MIT at 12 years old.. As an Ethnologist, he deciphered the Muian Language from the downed Mu Galaxy Cruiser stored at Area 51. Ryan traveled by Stargate with Anami Kordova and Gen. West to PX-338. Ryan was born in Calcutta, India.

Their Centaurians counterparts made ready to backup the Earth Territorial Fleet. The Officials were Capt. Elizabeth Harmony of the Solar Wind, Comdr. Ben Hur of the Nova and Capt. Ezar of the Shallum.

Leading the Special Unit Team was Lt. Comdr. Lori Dawson; her operatives were Cornell, Tenderhand and Steele. They were Humans who chose to remain on Centillion after being abducted as children by Dr. Q. and rescued by the Centaurians from Dr. Q's slave ship.

> "The adventure begins," Comdr. Hur sent a message to Capt. Mack and the Earth Fleet, as they rendezvoused at the coordinates light years outside of the Throx sensor array. "We are ready to assist if needed."

> "Let's hope there's not much of that," Capt. Harmony replied. She was Uridian, the blue-complexioned Female who married British Ambassador Stewart.
> "How did you get this assignment?" Capt. Mack whispered to Ambassador Stewart.
> "You know the answer to that, ole chap," he replied with a grin, "she made me volunteer; those Uridian females bossy and can't get enough, you know..."

"That's classified information..." Capt. Mack chuckled.

Capt. Mack sat in his Captain's Chair. He'd been given the chance of a lifetime. The past three years he'd gone through extensive training on how to operate a Starship. He was also surrounded by brave, professional, even alien beings of far more superior intelligence than himself; he had grown to trust them with his very life; others he handpicked from former combat missions in the toughest and meanest areas of the world. These were battle-tested soldiers who loved America.

"Capt. Harmony, beam your Security Unit aboard," Capt. Mack told her, feeling strange in saying such words, ordering a Centaurus Officer around; but this was his Mission. Yet he was still making the transition from Special Ops in Iraq and Afghanistan to Special Ops on distant planets and moons.

The SU Team were beamed aboard the Coral Sea.

"Engage Warp Drive, set Course to 222-Ulemen at Warp Factor 8," Capt. Mack continued.

The Coral Sea opened a vortex in the fabric of space entered and disappeared from the region. They were on their way to P-222 Ulemen.

THE GREEN LIGHT

A Special Meeting of the Synod of System Lords was called. Present were Anami Kordova, Emperor Vox, Premosee, and Wench-Desiree. The others declined for various reasons.

The room was large with a horse-shoe-shaped conference table. Anami stood before them. The mood was serious yet respectful and businesslike.

"Synod, as Leader of the System Lords," Anami began, "I went to Earth in pursuit of Kore. Through information gathered on Earth, it was discovered the Grand Exalted Ruler of Chud was financing the abductions and forced slavery of an estimated 5,000 Human Beings. I've personally seen the Symbios Pools on P-209, confiscated computer documents from Dr. Q, and interviewed the Human captives who slaved miserably maintaining the pools. The evidence was overwhelming; and now we have more evidence of Human Trafficking within the Domain."

"Are you proposing that we intervene, another military Correction?" Vox asked. " In the past, the GER has threatened war if any of us intruded into its Domain. Has our alliance with the Humans become a liability?"

"Emperor Vox," Anami replied, "Whether or not we had even heard of the Human Race or have a Treaty with them is not the issue; In the past we fought against such aggressive and immoral behaviors: The conquest of primitive civilizations like the Ulemens, and forced Symbios Implantations, the very actions that prompted the "Correction." We all know the GER is cruel and diplomatically unreachable. Of the GER will resist Correction. "

"I agree," Premosee said, "the Correction was a Just Cause, and present action should be taken."

"Thank you. So you see our alliance with the Humans isn't the issue. If the GER is allowed to enslave Humanoids----eventually implanting them with its Symbios, then he'll become our worst nightmare. The Symbios in the pools are identical to the one in Kore. How would you govern your peaceful worlds with 10 billion Alien Kores stalking the Milky Way Galaxy?"

"Point well taken" Premosee added, on the subject of Alien Kore---he remains at large and must be dealt with."

"It's my position that this extraction of Humans be accomplished without invoking a full-scale war," Wench-Desiree told him. "I lost nearly 500 soldiers during the last Correction. Do you have a feasible plan?"

"I appreciate your concern. The Centaurus Special Unit and Earth Territorial Fleet will work together."

"I want to be a voice of reason," Vox added, "The ETF are infants out here; keep them from being crushed or causing more problems than they solve. If you need assistance, you can count on me.

"You have my backing with one condition:" Wench-Desiree began, " If you get the chance, terminate the Grand Exalted Ruler. He's literally a monster, and quite an eyesore. By the way, how is Christina? Give her my love."

Anami walked over to the wall. He waved his right hand: The wall became a Dimensional Bridge. Anami steps through and was transported from the Council Room into his Mission Briefing Room. Present was Gen West and several members of the Joint Chiefs.

"The meeting with the Synod went well. The Synod agreed their National Security and interest is threatened. Together we'll be successful in liberating the Human captives without causing a war. As I explained earlier, our Battlestars are known to the GER's Throx Security Troopers. The ships you have aren't manufactured by the Empire but were confiscated during the Conflict. The Throx sensor nets are also programmed to detect Centaurians Genetic Markers. That's the reason only Humans will beam down to the planet."

"We'll leave in 12 hours," Gen. West said.

Anami Kordova, the System Lord opened a portal in the wall and left the room.

CHAPTER TWELVE
BIG MACK ATTACK

"Are you ready for more Frequent Flyer Miles?" Lt. Comdr. Dawson asked.

"Yeah, right," Capt. Mack responded, "if I got paid for the miles I've traveled I'd be a multi-billionaire. So, tell me about this Solar Storm."
"In the Domain this Cycle of the System, the sun erupts and sends solar flares throughout the Domain. This causes an interruption in long distance communications and sensor arrays. The plan is to sneak onto P-222, extract the Humans while the sun disturbance hides our presence from Throx Central Headquarters. The Throxs, as you already know are the hired security force of the Grand Exalted Ruler."

As they neared P-222 of the Delta Quadrant, Capt. Mack sat in anticipation to execute his orders. The landing Team was armed and ready, waiting in the Transporter Room and Cargo Bays. An eerie silence was in these rooms as the men and women reflected within themselves what would be needed from them to accomplish the mission and come back to their love ones alive and uninjured.

"Approaching P-222," Lt. Chavez announced, "we've dropped out of Warp. Throx Cruisers in fixed orbit!"

"Fire, proton missiles, medium spread," the Captain ordered.

The missiles hit and destroyed the Throx Cruisers without them knowing what happened who attacked them.

"That's my Big Mack Attack. They didn't see it coming. One moment they're sipping tea, and the next they're dead. Life is so temporary and riddled with unnecessary evils."

"Here comes his famous, "devils in the mountains" speech," Maj. Rice sighed.

"No, they moved to the suburbs of outer space!" Capt. Mack insisted, still proud of his ambush.

But the victory celebration was short lived. The Coral sea was violently shaken as though hit by debris.

"Status report, Capt. Mack requested.
"We're snagged by an automated defense system. It's Tractor Beams technology. I can't pinpoint it's exact locations, but there's several energy beams drawing us to the surface. Estimated impact is twelve minutes," Lt. Chavez told the Captain.

"Reroute non-essential power to engines. Reverse engines to full. Sound Collision Alarm. Brace for impact. All crew armed and ready to go. Lt. Comdr., have you seen anything like this before? Will this be a controlled landing or an actual crash?"

Collision Alarm sounded throughout the ship. Armed troops hurried to their stations and exit points.

"I've seen this technology, but we didn't know P-222 utilized it. Most likely the Throxs installed it as an upgrade. Just keep the engines reversed and the forward shields maxed-out. And expect the worst, but hope for something better. This type of beam coverage won't allow us to jettison escape pods or use the transporters. The good thing is they most likely want the ship and its contents intact."

"Orbit deteriorating rapidly. Hull temperature at 1,500 degrees and climbing. We're slowing down a little and the Shields are holding."

"I celebrated too soon. My first important mission and I lose my ship!"

" None of this is your fault. Our intel wasn't complete. We sent a Probe, not an actual ship."

When the ship landed the shielding was jammed. Twenty fully-armed Throxs transported onto the ship. The Intruder Alert Alarm sounded: "Intruder Alert on Deck Two!"

"Do they think this is a Greyhound Bus? It's full of Green Berets and Special Unit Soldiers. Go down there and kick their asses!" The Captain ordered.

On Deck Two, eight Throxs, armed with proton rifles, charge up the corridor. They pause only to look into the adjacent rooms. As they turn a corner, the Green Berets fired on them with modified M-4 weapons firing semi-noiseless projectiles. Three Throxs were immediately killed in the fight, the others retreat. Another group of Berets came up behind the retreating Throxs and throw Percussion Grenades at them. The grenades exploded and killed the remaining Throxs.

The Starship Coral Sea was forced down in a prepared clearance. Outside a Brigade of Throx vehicles surrounded the ship. The vehicles were equipped with missiles and phaser cannons. They appeared menacing and capable of penetrating even the hardest hull metals.

> "Are we held by the Tractor beams?" Capt. Mack asked Lt. Chavez.
>
> "No. They've switched to a magnetic field, like a giant magnet below the surface. We have an incoming message from Sub-Commander Are.
>
> "Surrender the ship, and I will spare your worthless lives!" Sub-Commander Are barked.
>
> "You're so kind to strangers," Capt. Mack told him. "Over the top, but to the point. So here is how this will play out: We can't go anywhere, but you can. Now, Lt. Chavez."

The vortex of a small hyperspace window opened in front of the Starship. It roared with deafening sound and swirled dark energy. The Throxs and equipment lifted off the ground. The Throxs screamed in terror as they and military hardware were sucked into the vortex; everal small animals, trees uprooted and disappeared into the vortex. Lt. Chavez terminated the hyperspace window.

The ETF, Green Beret Team combined with the Special Unit Team emerged from the ship and secured the perimeter. There were no other Throxs in sight.

"The ship is scorched but undamaged. My instruments detect an underground power station to the left of us. There's a hidden entrance," Lt. Chavez concluded.

"Take all but six of the team. We'll stay with the ship but move it in case more Throxs return," Captain Mack told them. "We'll be in full cloak and waiting for your signal."

The Team found a well-traveled path into the jungle in search of the power source that held the ship magnetically to the planet surface.

"What more can you tell me about the GER?" Maj. Rice asked Lt. Comdr. Dawson. The two had become good friends since being teamed together on Earth. Together they stormed the subterranean Cavern and defeated Alien Kore and Sanballat.

"Not too much more: As I stated earlier, it's asexual, and the oldest System Lord in the Delta Quadrant. His Domain was originally a water world until the sun enlarged, grew hotter and dried up the oceans. Now the GER is forced to breed in constructed pools.

"So Kore thought he was conquering Earth to become our System Lord, when in fact it was his GER-symbios that was actually driving him.

"Correct. The best we can profile, is that at times Kore actually thinks he's in control and making the decisions, when in fact he's only executing the will of the GER. Kore is a survivor, always has been; he's also a fighter. Some of us think there's still some good in him."

The Point Man motioned for everyone to stop. The Team crouched down. Two Throx sentries posted at the entrance to a bunker. The team, including Maj. Rice and Lt. Comdr. Dawson fired their weapons. They killed both Throx sentries. The team moved forward to secure the tunnel opening. Rice and Dawson stayed behind.

"You're look so hot when you fire your weapon," Maj. Rice told her. He had been wanting her for months.

"Then why all the GER questions, you want to date her or me?" She smiled, wantonly because she liked him."

Hidden by jungle growth they embraced and kissed. Moments later, a soldier came looking for them, saw them kissing and walked away shaking his head. trealized they had been discovered. The Officers joined the others as though nothing had happened. The bunker was connected to a tunnel.

The tunnel was bored into a mountain. It was dimly lit. The floor and walls were smooth, round, but the floor was flat. Bugs, spiders, rats and small rodents crawled on the floor and walls. An occasional snake crossed their path.

The squeaky sound of a door opening was heard. The team stopped, weapons aimed ahead. A animal roar sound was heard.

"What the hell was that?" Hall asked."

A Saber-Tooth Tiger raced towards them. The tiger was full grown and wore body armor. The Team fired their weapons but the bullets bounced off the armor. As the tiger got closer, Lt. Chavez, the snipe quickly put it down with a head shot. Then several Throxs emerged from adjacent rooms and attacked the Team from every side. The Team shot some, and hand-to-hand stabbed to death the others. Singlehandedly, Major Hall literally beat two of them to death. When the battle was over fifteen Throxs laid dead on the floor.

But as they went further into the bunker, another sound was heard. Loud footsteps. A large creature came towards them from deep within the bunker.

"Another Saber-Tooth Tiger?" Maj. Rice surmised.

"No, cats don't walk that heavy----maybe a bear," Pro. Shariyat surmised.

The creature appeared. It was seven foot tall, green and extremely muscular. It growled at them, picked up a huge boulder and threw it at the Team. They raced for cover. The boulder didn't hit anyone.

"If I didn't know better, I'd say we found the Incredible Hulk! The size of that beast?" Lt. Chavez proclaimed.

"Maj. Hall, the Incredible Hulk isn't a real creature," Pro. Shariyat, being analytical reminded him."
"I know that Professor…"
"It's call an Oz." Lt. Comdr. Dawson told them.

"Hulk or Oz. He's pissed off at us!" Hall added, "can you get a clear shot at it?"

"I can shoot anything."Maj. Chavez grinned.

"Don't shoot it, but keep it away," Pro. Shariyat insisted. "Maybe we can capture it for science,"

"You capture it!" Maj. Rice told him, "take it to school for Show-and-Tell all I care---but our mission is to rescue our people, not start a freak show!"

After laying down cover fire, Lt. Comdr. Dawson arrived at the control panel and switched the artificial gravity field off and released the Coral Sea. The others stood between the creature and the exit.

Lt. Comdr. Dawson destroyed the console so the equipment could not be used against them on departure, but hacked into the Throx computers and downloaded the information stored on it.

"There's a lot of information on this computer," Lt. Comdr Dawson told them, "Our destination lies five miles from here. Let's go."

The Team exited the bunker and headed out. They traveled on a well-used but muddy trail. Maj. Rice motioned for everyone to spread out and follow him; he was the Point Man. Travel was slow. The road was slippery with red clay mud that clung to their boots. Every now and then, they stopped and cleaned their boots.

Trampling through the jungle on both sides were hundreds of snarling creatures; some with cloven hoofs, paws and claws; there were also prehistoric winged reptiles circling above them. They growled and lunged to intimidate but none attack them.

They traveled down a trail that lead to a large clearing. At a distance rested 250 Throx War Cruisers. The Cruisers were being loaded by Throxs and Ulemens with racks of missiles and supplies, as though going on a long journey. In a distance stood thousands of "modified" Oz Creatures.

"What's going on here? "Maj. Rice asked Lt. Comdr. Dawson.

"That's exactly what I'm thinking. It's a Cyber-Oz---an Oz with visible implants, computer sensory enhancements and built-in weapons. We came across a few during the Correction---but there's at least 10,000 of them here."

"We must get this information to the Empire," Major Rice concluded, as said and took a video of the Throx Base.

BAT ROCK

Bat Rock was a small island off the Cameron Coast. The evening was gloomy. The clouds hung low. Gloom pervaded the souls of the people. Depression, fear and evil had subdued the Ulemens. All the happiness and bliss of a lifetime of peace and tranquility was taken from them the day the Grand Exalted Ruler of Chud set his sights on Ulemen for conquest.

"Make way!" An announcer declared.

Chief Rama and Xandi burst into the crowd. They pranced up the long velvet carpet that lead to their thrones. Beyond the thrones was an altar, a monument erected as a place to honor and worship the Grand Exalted Ruler of Chud, their new god.

The monument was 50ft. tall, clad with beaten gold and ornamented with precious jewels. At the core blazed an infernal; flames exploded out its mouth and smoking nostrils. Several Ulemens fed the fire with huge logs.

The couple satt themselves upon two stone and ivory jeweled thrones. The Chief raised his hand.

> "Ulemens, in honor of our Master, the most worthy Grand Exalted Ruler, who has opened our blind eyes to understand the mysteries of the stars, we offer tonight's sacrifices. Bring forth the virgins!"

Two young virgins, Humans, stood at the end of the carpet runway. The natives artistically painted the women with exotic inks. The females were forced to kneel at the Chief's feet and received his blessings, then they ascended the steps until reaching the top landing.

When Chief Rama nodded, the first woman was pushed off the landing into the inferno. The crowd cheered.

Without warning, artificial light bathed the small island as though an enormous spotlight came on. Lightning rent the clouds. The GER appears in front of Chief Rama. He was extremely angry at Chief Rama. The GER tapped his staff on the ground: Chief Rama ejected off his seat and landed face down in the nearby weeds.

> "Fool, what are you doing?!"
> "We're sacrificing virgins to worship you."
> "Worshipping me is an honorable deed, but I brought the Humans here to service my Spawning Pools---not for your purposes!"

Now the GER's voice changed into that of a loving and caring Female voice.

> "If you slay my children in your sacrificial fires, how will the Humans procreate to replenish their numbers in the Domain? I will be forced to enslave more of your people instead? The choice is yours."
> "I'll cease this practice; I'll do what you say?"
> "Excellent my child. Pick yourself up and stop this nonsense. Find some other evil to marinate in, but leave my Humans alone. If you have any questions about what or what not to do, ask Kore. He's my Enforcer."

The GER transported back to the Silver Hawk. Kore gazed upon the platform and saw a beautiful redhead.

> "Bring that woman to my house and treat her well," he told them.

That night, Penelope was brought into Kore's bedroom. She stood at the door. The moonlight shined on her silky naked body. She was a young, shapely woman about 20 years old. Kore sat up in the bed and gazed upon her beauty.

"Come in and let's get acquainted," Kore said in a soft and friendly voice. "Don't be afraid. You don't have to do anything unless you want to."

"I want to please you Kore," she replied.

Penelope came over to him. Kore reached out. She positioned herself on top of him, talking charge, and had intercourse with Kore. Over the years, this was not the first time she'd seen Kore but never spoke to him.

A week later, Kore sat at his table with Throx Comdr. Mar. He was in charge of the Throx forces on Ulemen.

"Have you discovered where that ship went that destroyed our two ships?" Kore asked him.

"My troops are searching as we speak, but with no success. It was likely Elam Pirates. They come when the solar storm is at its worst looking for things to steal. They most likely have left the planet."

"My future plans are bold and fiery. My expectations are extremely high. All you Throxs have to do is ride on my big shoulders!"

"We're working as fast as we can. You do want victory with no mistakes."

"Yes, I want Earth soil under my feet this time next year. I also want President Kensington's head in my trophy case."

"Rest assured, we'll corner the Earth leaders like rats and rip out their little hearts. We'll feed them to the Symbios!"

"I hope the other Throx Leaders are as cruel."

"But none are as cruel as you, Alien Kore. That's

why you serve at the GER's pleasure. It's your destiny to forever secure slaves for the Domain.
"But if I don't get victory" Kore points his finger at Comdr. Mar "---my final request before the GER kills me, is that I can kill you first!"

Pondering his own words, Kore suddenly looked cadaverous; his eyes glowed red and look hysterical; bitter anguish rested upon his lips. He stepped away as though ready to leave, but fell down on the marble floor. He convulsed and shook; then possessed by a demonic fit of rage, he pounded his fist against the floor until bloodied.

"I'll utterly crush them!" He raved. "I hate them!

Kore crawled back to his seat; he held his head in his hands, until the Symbios in his head quieted down. Drops of blood fell on the floor.

"Use as much Ulemen labor as needed to load the Cruisers. On your way out, send in Penelope. That is all for now."

Penelope came into the room., She was clean and well dressed; her long red hair was beautifully styled by the two female assistants that were assigned to her.

"Good Morning Penelope?
"Good Morning Kore, how is your day?"
"I've heard it said, "there's no rest for the wicked." But, otherwise, I'm surviving. Are the Ulemens and Throxs treating you well?"
"Yes, but my own people call me a whore, a Sex Slave of yours. Am I a Sex Slave or your woman?"

"You're my woman; they're just hating because they have to work and you don't."

"So I'm not just someone compatible to have sexual intercourse with? I'm Human, and you're close to Human, so it's only natural for you to want some fringe benefits.

"No, we have a real relationship; there's no one but you. I'm not with you only for sex---though it's been real good--- but I really like you; I really like being with you."

"Thank you. Hey, you're hurt. Let me bandage those hands. How did this happen---have you been fighting?"

"Fighting against myself. Thank you. It has been a while since anyone cared about me. I told you I was married but my wife was killed. Sometimes, you remind me of her. But in many other ways you are uniquely different.

Penelope sent for her maidens who brought in towels and a bowl of water. Penelope cleaned Kore's wounds.

"So, what makes me so special to deserve clean clothes, servants and a private room?"

"I think I have already answered that question. I will only add that I need a friend, someone I can trust. I like your company, in return I make your life easier; no more caretaking at the Symbios Pools; being yelled at or prodded by electrical rods. I'm in the position to give you a meaningful life and freedom."

"Then return me to Earth."

"Not that much freedom...not yet."

"Are you promising that you will someday return me to Earth?"

"I'm saying that changes are coming; these changes will affect both our lives. I'm going on a long voyage and want you to go with me."

"I will go anywhere with you. Kore, you're too nice a guy to be mixed up with these egomanias. The GER is a straight-up monster; the Throxs are crazy crocodiles, and the Ulemens are idol-worshipping fanatics; they tried to kill me. Ever think about quitting?"
"I think about quitting as much as I think about dying; in my world there's no difference between the two. And I'm not as nice as you think; there is a crazy monster side of me too."

THE ROAD TO GLORY

The team continued making headway down the muddy road. A massive hawk-like predator circled the sky overhead. It suddenly swooped down and sunk its talons into Pro. Shariyat's back. The impact made him drop his rifle. The predator's powerful wings created lift and picked the Professor off the ground and started to leave the trail with him.

"Somebody help me!" The Professor screamed in terror, thinking his next breath would be his last.

Lt. Chavez placed the hawk in his rifle sight. He shot the hawk in the head. The single head shot killed the creature. It plunges to the ground, tumbled a few times and released Pro. Shariyat. The professor only received scratches and abrasions from the fall and tumble. He wiped the mud from his face, and walked back to the Team.

"Are you okay?" Maj. Hall asked.

"Yes, but I screamed like a little girl. Fortunately my backpack stopped its claws. That was too close. Thanks Lieutenant for the help. I thought it was over for me."

"You're welcome," Lt. Chavez told him.

"Guess you don't want to capture that beast for science!" Maj. Hall chuckled.

"I wish we had time to roast this big chicken over an open fire," Maj. Rice added, "my stomach is chewing on my backbone!"

"Kentucky fried chicken-hawk---sounds like some good eating!" Lt. Comdr. Dawson added.

"I forgot for a moment that you're Human and originally from Earth," Pro. Shariyat told her."

"Yep, I still remember Fast Food. I heard there'll be several Earth Franchises on Centillion next year."

Suddenly the nearby creatures smelled the blood of the hawk. In great numbers they converged on the carcass. It so happened the dead hawk was between them and the objective. A fierce fight erupted over which creature would eat the hawk.

"They're blocking the trail," Maj. Hall stated.

The Team waited until the creatures finish eating the hawk. But instead of leaving the trail, the creatures charged the Team.

"Lock and load, things are about to get bloody!" Major Rice warned.

The Team responded with automatic fire. Their weapons brought down dozens of the stubborn beasts. Soon they were surrounded by savage creatures of diverse species, shapes and sizes. Energy Pulse Grenades were thrown to even the overwhelming odds. The team killed, wounded and drove back the assault.

> "We're making too much noise," Lt. Comdr. Dawson warned them. "We don't have a lot of time before the Solar Storm is over and the Throxs repair the equipment we destroyed. I'm sure they know we destroyed the Planet Sentries."

As she spoke, overhead, an Astral Sled glided over the treetops. It hovered over the sight of the animal slaughter. The large platform held six Throx Troopers. The Team darted unobserved into the jungle.

> "What's happened here?" The Throx Trooper said to the others. Why all the dead animals?"

He scanned the animal carcasses.

> "I detect the use of energy weapons and metallic projectiles," the Throx Trooper concluded. "We have intruders in this area. I must report this."

> "Fire at will, "Maj. Rice ordered.

The Team fired from their jungle hiding places. But their steel-jacked bullets and phaser beams deflect off the protective force shield surrounding the platform.

Lt. Comdr. Dawson opened her backpack and removed a silver orb. She activated it, tossed it up in the air. It hovered a moment, then attached itself to the

Astral Sled force field. The force field glowed bright. The sled disintegrated.

"No evidence," Comdr. Dawson stated.

"Instead of walking in all this mud, wish we could've used that platform. I am so tired. My boots weigh ten pounds each," Pro. Shariyat complained.

"We don't have an hour to bypass the Throx genetic link to operate the craft, plus all of us can't fit on it anyway. We have to stay together. This is a world similar to what Earth was like millions of years ago. You saw the Saber-tooth, Oz and giant hawk; I'm certain there are even larger creatures watching us."

"Okay, I understand."

As they proceeded closer to their objective, they evaded encounters with the Throx astral patrols. The sun was very hot. The atmosphere was thick with humidity. The Team cautiously trudged on while keeping a vigilant eye on the stalking animals and sky patrols.

The Point Man passed a group of large leafed plants thriving beside the road. One of the plants moved.

"Watch out Tenderhand!" Cornell warned, Cornell was usually quiet and seldom engaged in conversation, but this was an emergency.

One of the plants opened its bulb head, reached onto the trail and completely swallows Tenderhand.

Maj. Hall rushed over. The other team members opened fire and shot the lower portion of the plant near the ground, being careful not to hit the swallowed soldier. Hall withdrew her survival knife and jumped on the plant. She carefully plunged her knife into the green skin and cut it open. When she reached Tenderhand, the plant's powerful digestive acid reduced him to a skeleton in his tattered uniform. His boots were still smoking. Everyone was shocked and amazed.

Lt. Comdr. Dawson sadly viewed the remains of Spec. Tenderhand and it sickened her.

> "We're sorry about Tenderhand. He was a good soldier," Maj. Rice consoled her.
> "Yes he was; it's too bad. Tenderhand leaves behind a wife and two children. He married a Centaurian."

Lt. Comdr. Dawson stood over the remains of Tenderhand. Her mind recalled the circumstances that led to her first meeting him.

ABDUCTION

Toledo Ohio: Sherry Dawson stood in her living room at the bottom of the steps. She lived with her 10 year old daughter, Lori. Sherry was a single mother. She was middleclass, a Quality Control Inspector at the Ford Motor Company. Her home was neat and clean, furnished with quality furnishings; it depicted her good taste and class.

> "Hurry up Lori, the Video Store will be closed in ten minutes!"
> "I'm coming!"

Lori ran down the steps and to the front door. She was a high-energy child, full of spunk and sass.

" Let's walk," Lori insisted.
"Okay, it's only a few blocks."

Sherry and Lori walked the first block then took a shortcut across the neighborhood park. As they came upon a group of trees, two Mutant Grays step out from behind the trees. They were five feet tall with large heads and coal-black eyes. The aliens blocked their path by standing in front of them.

"Nice costumes, but Halloween is two months away," Sherry told them. "It's getting late, you kids need to go home. Do your parents know that you are out here?"

The Mutant Grays approached them. Sherry stepped back and clutched Lori's hand. A Mutant Gray pulled out a weapon and stunned them.

The next thing Sherry and Lori knew they were in Earth Orbit aboard a Mu Galaxy-Class Cruiser. Lori was strapped to a cold stainless steel table. She was being thoroughly examined. Sherry wasn't in the room. Next to her was a male child. Both were fully conscious.

"These children are perfect for my Symbios program," Dr. Q said. "Very healthy. Put them with the others children."

A Mutant Gray released the leather straps holding the children. The same Mutant Gray took them by the hand and out of the Examination Room.

"What's your name?"" Lori asked the boy.
"Michael Tenderhand. I'm from Houston, Texas"
"I'm Lori Dawson from Toledo, Ohio"

THE SPAWNING POOL

The Team came upon what appeared to be the end of the planet. The trail abruptly ended at a sheer cliff. A hazy sky stretched for hundreds of miles. At a distance winged prehistoric predators were seen. The only place to go was down.

"This makes the Grand Canyon look like a pot-hole!" Pro. Shariyat gasped.
"Our forced landing took us miles away from our objective," Lt. Comdr. Dawson confided. "Plus the solar flares distorted our instruments; but if we had ventured to close the Throxs would have picked us up; a cloaked ship will still move air around."
"That's because it's not in another dimension," Pro. Shariyat added."
"Correct, it only bends light and distorts space."

The Team lined up at the edge of the cliff and dove off. They freefell for a minute then the anti-gravitational units on their utility belts slowed their descent, until they cruised to a comfortable landing.

After walking another hour, they arrived at their destination. Through binoculars, the Team viewed the Compound. The meat processing building was where the Throx Hunters took the wild game to be processed for the Symbios, Throx and Human consumption.

Next to that building was the Pumping Station with large diameter steel water lines that lead to the massive Symbios Spawning Pools. There were six buildings, including barracks. Human Beings worked around the pools, under the watchful eyes of mean-looking Throx guards.

Near the Pumping Station were constructed housing units adjacent to concrete-reinforced bunkers where the Throxs lived. Phaser Gatling guns protruded from the slotted windows. As the team looked around the camp, near the jungle edges loomed two antiaircraft guns and two surface-to-air missile platforms rested. Next to that was a Throx Combat Cruiser. There was movement in and out of the Main Gate so the Shield Generator was not activated.

> "Damn!" Was all Major Rice could say.
> "It's a hundred times larger than I imagined," Lt. Comdr. Dawson added.
> "Look over by the Throx Cruiser: It's Dr. Q." Maj. Rice pointed.
> "No, it will take all the fun out of it." Maj. Chavez told him.

The Throxs were on vigilant alert for intruders. Nevertheless, the Humans labored feverishly throughout the Compound; they filled buckets of meat scraps from a large conveyor and emptied them into the Symbios Pools. The pools were very large. As usual, the hungry Symbios jumped and flopped about in the pool like Salmon going upstream as they feasted on the raw meat.

"The the solar winds have ceased…"

Lt. Comdr. Dawson leaned over to look. She touched Maj. Rice's hand as she took the device from it. Their eyes met, as though they wanted to kiss.

"You have seen well, grasshopper," she said with a smile.

A minute later, Capt. Mack and the Starship Coral Sea materialized above the Compound.

"Beam up the Humans," he calmly ordered, "including our Team."

The Human slaves and the Strike Team were beamed into the Cargo Hold of the ship. When seeing the Coral Sea, the Throxs immediately fired upon it with small arms while others rushed to operate the heaver weapons and board the Cruiser. By the time they made it to the weapons, the Coral Sea accelerated towards the clouds. It was out small arms range. They readied the surface-to-air missiles.

"Did you get everything you needed Professor Shariyat?" Capt. Mack asked.
"Yes sir, Every scrap of information from the Throx Computer Grid."
"Fire Aft Missile Launchers 1-8."

The Proton Missiles left through the rear launchers of the Coral Sea. The first missile landed within 5 feet of Dr. Q. He disintegrated. The others hit the Compound and Cruiser. Both Throxs and Symbios vaporized.

"Major Rice, you have the Chair."

Capt. Mack left the Bridge and went to the Cargo Hold. There he visited the recently liberated people. He spent an hour talking with them, then, being tired, went to his quarters. As soon as he fell on the bed he went to sleep. He dreamt of one of his many war adventures:

2008, Earth, Kabul Afghanistan: When a Major, Mack recalled the nightmare of his capture by the Taliban. He received intel that a local shop owner had information about a High Priority Target the U.S. wanted to eliminate. The owner would only talk to him. He sat in a small shop, his driver and a soldier waited outside in the truck.

Unknown to him, two Taliban Fighters crept up on his men, cut their throats and dragged them into the side alley. Then they went in the back door of the shop.

The owner of the shop came out the back room. With him were the two Taliban Fighters with AK-47 Assault Rifles. They took Maj. Mack's weapon. The other hit him over the head with the butt of his rifle. Maj. Mack crashed to the floor and fell unconscious.

Moments later, a rusted-out truck pulled into the alley. The Taliban Fighters loaded Maj. Mack into the bed of the truck and tied him up. The truck sped down a dirt road three miles from town. There the two Taliban Fighters took the Major out of the truck and dragged him into a tent.

Hours on end he was subjected to interrogation and torture by the two. He hung, naked by his wrist in a tent. One of the torturers threw a bucket of water on him. The other picked up the ends of battery jumper cables that were connected to a stack of batteries. He touched the ends together and it made a big spark.

"You're Special Forces, correct? Tell me, where are the locations of your teams? Tell me, and I'll spare your life," the Taliban Fighter asked.
"My men are at your mother's house, taking a turn with her!"
"You think this is all a joke I want you to know one thing: I hate Americans!"

The torturer shocked Maj. Mack. He yelled in excruciating pain; he fell unconscious. The other torturer threw water in the. Major's face and woke him up.

Maj. Mack noticed this torturer was real close. He wrapped his legs around the man's neck and gave a sudden jerk; he snapped the Taliban's neck. The weight of the two men snapped the wood beam at the top of the tent. Both men fell to the floor. On the way down Maj. Mack kicked the remaining Taliban Fighter. This caused him, jumper cables in hand, to fall face down in a puddle of water. With the cables under him, he jerked around in the water puddle as he was being electrocuted.

Maj. Mack freed himself from the ropes. He grabbed both AK-47 Assault Rifles and went to the door of the tent. Hearing the commotion and seeing the fallen tent, four Taliban fighters headed his way. The Major gunned them down. He jumped in the old rusty truck and took off down the road. There was no one left alive to chase him. This was the beginning of his Big Mack Attacks.

Capt. Mack awakened. He sweated. He sat up in bed and drank from a water glass. This recurring nightmare haunted him for years. Though he managed to get away from the Taliban, the horrors of that day and the lost of two young American Soldiers, would always be with him. Now he was Captain of the most powerful vessel known to mankind, a Starship.

But whether on Earth or in the cosmos, Evil thrived and lurked. Death and destruction found its way into every civilization. Hell was available and had enlarged itself to accommodate the evil geniuses and their followers for a final resting place.

The Grand Exalted Ruler was no different than the Earth tyrants who throughout Human History---the Adolf Hitlers--- controlled and murdered the innocent, have exterminated, enslaved and dehumanized their own people and those they deemed inferior, born to be subdued, exploited or destroyed through genocide, until bystander looked upon the misery, the degradation, could no longer be silent, and decided to do something about it.

CHAPTER THIRTEEN
I'M BACK!

It was a sunny day in New Mexico. It was 11:00 Saturday Morning and Gen. West was sleeping in with her female Life Partner. Toi was a young Caucasian blonde. She was also a runway fashion model.

"Good Morning Toi," Gen. West greeted. She kissed Toi on the lips. "I have to go to D.C., but I'll be back as soon as I can."

"Thought we were going to lunch and a movie?"

"I know, but I received an urgent message from the President."

"All work and no play?"

"We played a lot this weekend. Being on Call on Earth and Centaurus, it looked like a ghost town down there with nothing going on, until you came into my life."

"Just go to work….from now on, I'll take care of things down there…"

"I'll make reservations for you in Washington. I love you Toi."

"I love you more…"

In Washington D.C. there was a meeting of the Joint Chiefs of Staff with President Kensington in attendance: Gen. West, Sec. of Defense, Peace plus ten Generals and Admirals were in attendance.

Anami Kordova, the System Lord walked through the wall into the room. Anami stood in the middle of the room. He was dressed in his System Lord Robe.

"How does he do that?" One of the Generals whispered to another.

"Greetings from Centaurus. I apologize for this form of entrance. First, the captive Humans were rescued by your ETF and taken to Centaurus for medical treatment. They will be returned to you via Stargate tomorrow Morning."

Everyone applauded.

"Now the bad news: A Throx Armada of at least 250 Cruisers are heading your way. This was not because of the ETF raid, because the Throxs were already underway with the invasion plan when the ETF got there. We don't know exactly when they'll arrive at Earth, but with their fastest ships, it won't be less than three months."

"Can the Throxs be reasoned with?" Pres. Kensington asked hopefully.

"No. From our previous encounters with the Throxs, they are opportunist, ruthless and single-minded. Therefore, negotiation is out of the question."

"Isn't there a relationship between the GER and the Throxs," Gen, West asked.

"Yes, there's a Symbios agreement between the Throxs and the GER; they are willing hosts."

"Is there anything that the Empire can do to intercept the Invasion?" Pres. Kensington asked.

"They have too much of a head start for us to catch them. They would be at Earth at least a week before we arrive. By then Earth could be reduced to rubble."

"How is Kore's mental state. He wants to be our System Lord, do you think we can stall him until you get here?" Gen. West asked.

"Kore isn't in charge: The Grand Exalted Ruler wants to annex Earth into his Domain. He needs your oceans, hosts, servants---even worshippers. He's using Kore to accomplish it. Negotiating---to use a Human saying---that ship has sailed."

"Then America will immediately go on High Alert," the President concluded, " the NATO allies will be informed; the Russians and Chinese will undoubtedly be onboard, since if we fall, they'll be next."

"The 90th Space Wing and NORAD will continuously scan outer space. We are using the technology we used to discover the position of the cloaked Heavy Metal. Our space-based Infrared System of electronic listening devices and sensors are operational on most of the planets and moons," Gen. Obama told him.

"We have to work with what you have readily available, " Anami responded. "Your land- based systems are fine, but they can't take the battle to the Throxs. If the Throxs make it to Earth, from orbit they'll destroy your major cities and millions will die. But I do have a plan..."

"I think America is the first place Kore will attack," Pres. Kensington said.

"I agree. He's especially fond of you all."

TAKING A SHORT CUT

Aboard Throx Cruiser #5 as it crossed the vastness of space, Kore and Penelope were in the Captain's Quarters. It seemed they couldn't get enough of each other. This time Kore penetrated Penelope from the be-hind position until the vigorous lovemaking was over. Then she laid beside him. Kore kissed her passionately.

"That was great," Kore whispered. You have be-come an extraordinary love maker."
"Really? I didn't have any experience. I was a virgin when we met. You taught me everything."
"Believe me, I had a self interest in teaching you those tricks. It takes a lot to satisfy me."
"I know, sweetie, but I feel complete and satisfied when I'm with you. Kore, when will you tell me where we're going?"
"I told you: To visit friends. As you can see, they live far away, and it's hard to find the time to travel; plus the fuel prices these days."
"You make it sound like this Cruiser runs on gasoline. My father used to complain about fuel prices. I don't know a lot about Cruisers or space travel, but I know that this ship doesn't run on gasoline."
I was making a joke about Zutonium Crystals. But—never mind, the GER is paying for this trip so enjoy it. How old were you when you left Earth?"
"I was six years old."
"So it's been a long time without your parents."
"I barely remember them. But if the GER gives you a paid vacation, I guess you should take advantage of it and visit friends. Your frie-nds will be happy to see you, because you were considerate enough to spend months of your time, travel millions of miles to see them. One day I'll reunite with my family. I wonder what

Earth looks like after all these years? Who would still remember the little girl I was with the red braids that the boys in class pulled on. Did I tell you that I lived on Elm Street in Charleston, West Virginia?"

"No, you never told me that before. And yes, my friends will roll out the red carpet for me."

"I wish that I can convince you to settle down, get married and have children," she said.

"There will be plenty of time for love, romance and marriage. But first, as I said, I have to see my friends."

The Symbios in Kore's head gave him an electric shock. Kore closed his eyes because of the pain. He held his head in his hands. Penelope ran her fingers through his hair to soothe him.

"Can't you take something to stop the pain? With all this technology at your disposal, you don't have medication for a headache? On Earth we have over-the-counter remedies for headache pain."

"We also have pain relievers. I've tried everything. But the strong ones make me tired and sleepy; I can't do my job. Remember, there's a Symbios living inside me; it's the source of the pain. Me loving and caring for you makes the Symbios angry. We'll talk later."

Kore got up, got dressed and went to the Bridge. But on the way he mumbled:

"So sweet but yet so naïve…"

Throx Cruiser#5 and the other Cruisers in the Armada remained cloaked but dropped out of warp. Kore sat in the Captain's Chair. Other Throxs were at their posts. The Armada approached the Knox Space Station, a lone outpost guarded an extra-galactic Space Bridge. It was a new Supergate large enough for ships to pass through. Next to the gate was a Toll Space Station. Two Toll Booth Patrol Vehicles parked beside it.

"We're at the Knox Space Station. It appears the Space Bridge is operating. Awaiting your orders," Throx Comdr. Mar told Kore.

Coming this way was a gamble that paid off. Sources informed Kore that it would be functional. The Space Bridge between the Alpha and Delta Quadrants would trim months off their voyage. The Space Bridge folded up 75 trillion miles of space/time. And Earth was 108 trillion miles from Planet Chud.

"The Knox hate us," Comdr. Mar offered.
"Who doesn't hate us?" Kore replied, "face it, the Throxs and the GER aren't the most likable species in the universe; but personally, I'm not looking for friendships."

Four Throxs materialized inside the Command Center of the Space Station. They immediately killed the six operators then disappeared. Two proton missiles destroyed the Toll Booth Police Cruisers. Throx Cruiser#5 cloaked, and single file the 250-ship Armada crossed the Space Bridge into the Alpha Quadrant. Next stop: P-225 Earth.

CHIKERE

P-225 Earth, Headquarters of the Earth Territorial Fleet, Roswell New Mexico: This was formally Area 51. It was expanded to become the largest military base in the world. It was located in the New Mexico desert.

The Stargate that was once packed away in the warehouse, then placed in service by the Centaurians, was brought out and lifted by Hercules Helicopter and placed on one of the 25 runways. Hundreds of U.S. Military and Centaurians worked around the clock to ready America for the upcoming invasion.

Centaurian Scientist Chikere, an energetic female worked with Gen. West and the Earth Coalition which included the brightest scientists and engineers.

> "Our goal is to expand your Stargate. We'll dismantle it and materially combine it with several others to build a Space Bridge," Scientist Chikere told the General.
> "Sounds complicated, but show us what to do and we'll do it," Gen. West replied.
> "Yeah," she laughed, "it's complicated because a Stargate isn't made out of wood. It's metals are not found in this sector of the solar system."
> "What also a mystery is not knowing how much time that we have to complete it," Gen. West added.
> "Don't worry. Go home, get some rest. Spend some time with your family. There's nothing else you can do here. Remember, we has the element of surprise; Kore doesn't know we know he's coming."

I will rest once I see this will work. There's no point going home; I'll be calling you every ten minutes."

"I know, but I wouldn't answer. If my husband and children were here, they would have already called me fifty times." Waiting is always difficult, especially for those who think a lot or over-think things."

"I'm under a lot of pressure: Married to the Military. Special Operations has been my life for over twenty years! I can't see doing anything else. How long have you been married and how many "kids" you have?

"I presume that you mean children and not goats," she laughed. "My Universal Translator doesn't yet know the meaning of many slang words. We Centaurian don't speak English or any of the Earth Languages. We all have a Universal Translation Device implanted inside an ear; it's always learning and upgrading. Anyway, I've been married fifteen years and have three children. My husband is a Centaurian Diplomat."

"What does he and your children think about you going on this dangerous assignment?"

"Before I left, they baked me a cake which said: SAVE EARTH. That sums it up."

After hours of welding, rewiring and calibrating, they connected the Control Console and massive electrical cables to the Space Bridge. Chikere configured the 225-P-Address and they were ready.

Chikere dialed the Centillion address and the Space Bridge activated with a "swish!" sound. The gate, once round, was now large and oval-shaped., so the Event Horizon was shaped accordingly.

After she entered the Security Code, the first of many VXT Interceptors came through the Space Bridge. They immediately went skyward to clear the security fence at the end of the runway. Then in succession, a total of 100 Centaurian VXT Interceptors were on Earth. This was followed by hundreds of robot-operated tank-like armor vehicles sporting huge phaser cannons, missiles and Phaser Gatling guns. The Space Bridge stayed activated for hours, bringing weapon systems and personal.

In major cities throughout America, the Centaurian, military and civilian personal shipped and installed anti-spacecraft weapons atop buildings, open fields, upon factories, warehouses and near high priority targets, including the White House and Pentagon buildings. Alien technology weapons were installed on the military bases, ships and aircrafts.

CHAPTER FOURTEEN
REVENGE SERVED COLD

Earth, Cheyenne Mountain Colorado was the home of NORAD. Targets appeared on the long-range sensor networks. Gen. Obama and the NORAD group of military officers, advisors, specialists and scientists were called in to evaluate the sightings.

> "General, we have multiple targets on our long range sensor net. The objects are cloaked and at too great a distant to get exact numbers, a Technician reported."
>
> "Bring the Hubble Telescope around. Let's take a closer look," the General responded. "We outfitted her with new technology since Kore's last attack."

The Hubble Telescope was maneuvered by remote control to track and photograph the targets in that section of space. The Hubble Telescope computer digitally enhanced photos appeared on the view screen. It showed the Armada a faint outline of the cloaked ships.

> "It's the Throx invasion. Looks to be as Anami warned us. I will inform the President."

STATE OF THE UNION

At the White House, President Kensington, his cabinet members, Joint Chiefs, members of Congress and several news agencies were in the White House for

President's State of the Union Address. President Kensington entered from a side door.

"The President of the United States. All rise," The announcer beckoned.

"An hour ago NORAD's long range sensors detected the approaching Throx invasion fleet. We estimate that there are over two hundred ships. However, our friends the Centaurian—though living too far away to directly assist us, have loaned us formable weapons and strategies to defeat the Throxs. It's imperative that we take the battle to the Throxs, otherwise they may attack our cities from outer space causing tremendous loss of life. Our Constitution gives our citizens the right to bear arms. Yes, the military will be spread out equally to protect the entire nation. That's where you, the citizens come in: Recently, I signed an Executive Order for the Military, American firearm manufacturers and retailers to distribute, free of charge, firearms and ammunition to anyone over the age 18 who wants weapons to protect themselves, family and America. I have also signed a similar Executive Order concerning food, water and over-the-counter-medical supplies. This should eliminate panic. Fight the good fight of Faith; and may God bless America."

The President's Executive Order was immediately carried out in all the major cities. The military, U.S. Marshalls, F.B.I., Police Commissioners and Police Chiefs implemented the Order.

Warehouses and Semi trucks of weapons were already made available, driven into the population areas and dis-

distributed. Tanks and armored vehicles dotted the streets; the Army and American Red Cross sat up M.A.S.H. clinics to help the hospitals deal with foreseeable wounded.

As invasion time grew near, all private vehicles were ordered off the streets, and barricades were erected in strategic areas.

His Armada was now between Earth and Mars. Kore and Comdr. Mar were on the Bridge.

"Commander, send a message to Earth on their frequencies. The message: I'M BACK! When in range---you know what to do. President Kensington and America will go down first. After we destroy America, the rest of the world will surrender; one country, one fight, one victory."

Once in range, proton missiles were fired at the Hubble Telescope, International Space Station and several military and civilian telecommunication satellites. The results was complete obliteration.

The 200 VXT Interceptors materialized. They immediately fired on the Throx Cruisers. The multiple phaser cannons on the Cruisers returned fire. The VXTs zipped around the Cruiser fire and continued pounding the Armada. Several Cruisers were badly damaged on the first pass.

Kore almost wet his pants. He stood on his feet with his jaw hanging open. But his Bridge crew were too busy fighting off the VXTs to even notice him.

"Where did those VXTs come from? They're Empire Interceptors! Do they have a base here? Did the Empire knew we were coming? Two can play this game: Launch the T-105 Interceptors. We may make good of this yet. Our T-105s outnumber the VXTs three-to-one. It's going to take more than a few VXTs to stop us. All Captains get ready to transport the ground troops!"

"One thing in our favor, I don't see any Empire Warships in the vicinity," Comdr. Mar added.

The battle rages between the VXT Interceptors and the T-105 Interceptors. These VXT were automated weapons, whereas the T-105 has a Throx pilot. The VXTs got the upper hand in the battle because they were computer operated and had quicker reflects. The Throx edge was swiftly diminished to a hundred T-105s

The secret weapon attributed to the success over the T-105s was at NORAD. In a separate room was a sophisticated remote control chair. From this reclined chair, an alien, blue-colored Uridian child---9 years old boy--- controlled the VXT Interceptors. He saw the battle in space through integrated three-dimensional holographic images, produced by the cameras aboard the VXTs. The child was mentally capable of controlling the outcome of multiple battle locations at once. To him it was like playing a video game.

As the Throx Cruisers fought their way closer to Earth, Twelve Space Platforms appeared from their cloaked positions in outer space. A hundred and forty-four nuclear missiles with international insignias launched from the platforms.

Nuclear missiles hit the Throx Cruisers, but not before they transported their troops to Earth. Over a hundred Cruisers exploded; many others were damaged to the extent that the VXT Interceptors finishes them off. Only ten Throx Cruisers remained, while the remaining T-105s sped to Earth with the VXTs in hot pursuit.

On the Bridge, Kore viewed the Forward Screen as Throx Cruisers exploded around Throx Cruiser#5, leaving a large debris field to maneuver around. He was devastated. His eyes glowed red as he barked out orders to his Bridge crew, the Captains of the Throx Vessels and the leaders of the ground assault.

> "It's not as bad as it looks," Comdr. Mar told Kore. "The landing party is inflicting mayhem and fear. Our troops are in Washington D.C. The U.S. Capitol will be taken before morning."

> "Damn Americans---so unpredictable," Kore signed. The evil Symbios gave him a little time to be himself before the next strike.
> "And resourceful," Comdr. Mar added.

EYES OPENED WIDE

Frightened, bewildered and terrified, Penelope stumbled to the Bridge to see what was going on. She looked in horror at the view screen. She saw Earth attacked by the man she loved.

> "How could you do such a thing?!" She cried "You never told me we were coming to Earth, let

alone to attack it! Those are my people down there. How could you be so cruel? How could you deceive me like this! You used me all this time. You never loved me---it was only sex and lies!"

Kore came to his feet.

"I do love you. It hasn't been all a lie. My return to Earth and this battle is to become the System Lord. I don't expect you to understand."

Angrily, Penelope stepped toward Kore.

Kore presses a button on his utility belt. Penelope transported to Charleston West Virginia, onto the sidewalk in front of her house. In shock, she climbed the steps to the porch. She saw her mother through the bay window. She rang the doorbell and waited. Her mother opened the door.

"Hello Ma...it's me, Penelope."
"Oh, my baby! Come in!"

NORAD officials watched the battle while being protected in the granite mountain.

"The Hubble, Space Station and several military satellites are either inoperable or destroyed, I'm rerouting signals through the Mars and Moon networks."

"To think the D.O.D. almost denied us funds for this network," Gen Obama said, "After the first invasion, they didn't think lightning would strike twice in the same place. Kore probably doesn't feel so superior about now."

"No sir, he probably doesn't," the Specialist nodded. "Sir, more Transporter traffic from the Throx Cruisers over Washington DC. The remaining Throx Interceptors have broken through the outer perimeter. Their trajectory is Washington D.C. The VXTs are in pursuit."

"The ground war has begun," the General replied

In Washington D.C T-105 Interceptors roared across the sky. They encounter U.S. Air Force aircrafts, ground-based missile systems and the ant-spacecraft Gatling gun emplacements.

Throx and Cyber-Oz troops transported to the D.C. streets. The powerful Cyber-Oz fired their built-in wrist weapons. With their bare hands, they turned over trucks and armored vehicles for the Throxs to hide behind and fight. The Cyber-Oz went into buildings, shooting people or physically picking them up and throwing them around like ragdolls. Physically, the people couldn't defend themselves against the Cyber-Oz unless they shot them several times or with a high-powered weapon.

A Cyber-Oz cornered a teenager in an alley. He approached to kill her. She was visibly frightened, shaking in terror at being beaten to death..

"Don't make me have to chase you, Human. You can't escape me. Why don't you make it easy on yourself. I promise that I'll make it quick."

The Cyber-Oz also had a Symbios who spoke. A policeman arrived. He saw the girl confronted by the Cyber-Oz. and came to her rescue.

"Hey ugly! Why don't you get me instead!"
"Why not, two are better than one."
"Depends on what it is---how about six bullets?"
The Policeman countered.

The Cyber-Oz raises his right arm to fire his weapon. The Police Officer withdrew his weapon at lightning speed, like a practiced Old Western gunslinger; he fanned the hammer and fired his .44 Magnum weapon. The Cyber-Oz clutched his chest. He looked down in amazement at the six tight-patterned holes in his chest. The Cyber-Oz fell on a trashcan and smashes it. The Policeman reloaded his revolver.

"Come on young lady. Let me get you to safety."

Several Cyber-Oz were killed at close range by a 50 caliber machine gun with armor-piercing bullets. The soldier was in a barricade on Pennsylvania Avenue down the street from the White House. Gen. West and Sci. Chikere were also present. They were on their way to a shelter when the attack came.

"I downloaded the Throx technical data into the computer of the Dampening Field Generator. This jammed the Cyber-Oz circuitry and shut down the implants so their weapons don't work."
"Good because it's getting ugly out here in these streets. The body count on our side is mounting. I don't know if we're winning or losing. About now, I bet you wish you stayed home."
"General, Empress Christina is from Earth. She has family and friends here. What's important to her is important to me. Life has to include something, a cause or someone that each person is

willing to die for. This is my moment in destiny, my finest hour."

The armed civilians made this a good fight. They ambushed the Throx from their hiding places atop buildings, behind vehicles and dumpsters. Hundreds were so daring as to climb down into the storm sewers and fire their weapons out the curb openings. By the hundreds, Throxs laid dead in the streets. Crashed T-105s and a few VXTs dotted the landscape.

From Orbit, Throx Cruiser #5 fired two proton missile. They hit the White House. The missiles explode with a tremendous sound. The dome was completely blown away, and the remainder burned uncontrollably.

Another Throx Cruiser bombarded the Supreme Court Building and Library of Congress with missiles. Several proton missiles hit the Pentagon, located in Virginia just outside of D.C. The last missile was a ground-penetrating missile. It descended deep below the surface to the bunkers, then exploded. Debris jetted 1000 ft. in the air. The Pentagon becomes a pile of rubble.

The military bases and runways of several U.S. bases were simultaneously attacked to prevent further aircraft from taking off or returning to them for fuel and ordinance.

In the Atlantic Ocean off the East Coast, NATO Carriers and battleships equipped with conventional and nuclear missiles, launched ordinance into outer space at the orbiting Throx Cruisers and T-105 Interceptors.

In swift retaliation, several NATO carriers were hit by missiles and either sank or were incapable of continuing in the war effort. Military ships, helicopters and civilian ships aided in the rescue of sailors.

Modified ICBM nuclear missiles launched from their silos and attacked the orbiting Throx Cruisers. Twelve B-2 Spirits loaded with nuclear missiles ran high-altitude sorties against the orbiting Throx Cruisers with moderate success.

Believing they had D.C. under their belt, from orbit, the Throxs targeted the Empire State Building, Trump Building and New York Times Buildings for destruction. These buildings had anti-spacecraft and missile systems on the roofs. The Empire State Building was cut in half by the forward phaser of a Throx Cruiser. The debris tumbled down into the streets and a caused a hundred deaths, injuries and panic. Other buildings were also destroyed by proton missiles; flaming debris scattered for five miles.

Again from orbit, the Throx fired missiles and hit Trump International and the AT&T Buildings. These buildings also had anti-spacecraft and missile systems on the roofs. The buildings came down violently into the streets. Other building were randomly targeted and destroyed.

One Emergency Room was full of injured and dying people. The majority of them suffered from phaser burns or debris. A dozen of them got shot be either the military or civilian friendly fire.

The door opened. A wounded Throx stumbled in. The patients were surprised but stayed calm.

"Fix me!" The Throx demanded.

"Fix you?" A Doctor asked, "I don't know what you are. Are you a reptile? We don't have talking reptiles on Earth. I'm not a Veterinarian."

"There's won't to be talking reptiles where I'll send you: If I don't feel better soon, you've be practicing medicine in the afterlife! Now, take this piece of metal out of my back. And don't try anything suspicious!"

The Doctor walked cautiously to the counter to get forceps. The Throx turned around to eye the patients. Most were on their feet with guns out. They shot the Throx 10 times. He died in a hail of bullets.

A Throx kicked down the door of a private home. He and another entered the home. A Grandmother and her Granddaughter sat on the sofa. They listened to the radio broadcast of the fighting.

"We're hungry, the Throx Lt. barked, " Give us some food!"

No one moved. The Throxs went into the kitchen. Throx Lt. opened the refrigerator but found nothing that he wants to eat. He opened the freezer and grabbed a raw pork roast. He bit into the package. He threw the frozen roast through the kitchen window, breaking the glass. The roast bounced on the ground.

"There's another refrigerator in the basement. I thawed several steaks this morning," the Grand-mother advised, "help yourself."
"That's more like it," Throx Lt. gleamed, licked his lips with his crocodile tongue.

The Throxs went down the steps into the basement. The basement was small but there was an old refrigerator at the bottom of the steps

"Go outside Dawn, the Grandma said.
"Okay, Grandma," she replied.

Grandma took two grenades out her purse. She pulled the pins and throws them into the basement. Then Grandma hobbled to the side door and outside. The grenades bounced down the steps and stopped at the feet of the Throxs. The grenades exploded and killed both Throxs.

"Those Throxs are dumb as a box of rocks," Grandma told her. "I'm ninety years old and sharper than they are!"
"I can't wait until things get back to normal. Do you think the war will last long?"
"We beat them the last time and we'll beat them again."

At NORAD, Pres. Kensington and Top Government Officials monitored the view screen.

"The enemy T-105s are destroyed, and thanks to Scientist Chikere, the Cyber-Oz no longer has the use of their bionics; the last of them are being cornered and eliminated."
"Sir! Now we have a hundred new vessels entering our sensor net," a the Technician interrupted.
"A second wave. Kore held back half his Armada. I thought we received the full brunt of his forces. This drastically changes things," Gen.

General Obama sighed. "

"Surrender is not an option," President Kensington told everyone. "Contact the Chinese and Russian Federation. Inform them that we may not prevail this second wave. Tell them we fought the good fight!"

"Yes we did and we'll continue to fight!" I heard that you're a praying man, I suggest you pray with me now," Gen. Obama said, "we need a miracle."

"Stop all this doom and gloom," Shawn, the Uridian child told them. "All is not lost..."

"How would you like to be President during this crisis?" He asked the child.

"I'm only a child....but I know the sun will come out tomorrow ..."

"I guess we momentarily lost our Faith," Pres. Kensington nodded and took the child's hand.

CHUD

Delta Quadrant, P-023 Planet Chud, Talon City: Fifty Empire Battlestars and a hundred Battle Cruisers from Emperor Vox, Wench-Desiree and Lord Premosee grouped in fixed positions. In minutes they pulverized the major Provinces of Chud, killing millions of the GER's Symbios. While the majority of Throx forces were at Earth killing innocent Humans, they left the Domain Home World vulnerable to attack.

The Battlestars Andromeda, Shallum, Nova and Solar Wind; Starships Coral Sea, Eisenhower, Constitution and Victory joined in the assault on Chud.

The Silver Hawk with the GER aboard tried to take off, but the Silver Hawk was hit and damaged beyond repair. The GER fled to its underground lair.

After a devastating thirty-minute assault, the Synod beamed to the planet to confront the GER if he was still alive. His abode was underground in a cavern. They appeared before him.

"What is the meaning of this assault, this intrusion in my Domain? I warned all of you that if you entered my Domain I would severely punish you. Now you have murdered my Symbios and will pay dearly for it,"

"We're not gnats that you can shoo away when annoyed with us. You have engaged in Human Trafficking and attacked our ally on the Planet Earth. Plus, I don't like you and came for your head," Anami flatly told her.

"My head, Kordova, you have been reading your own publicity. I'll kill you then make the others eat your flesh."

"They're only here for the official record to witnesses the death of a System Lord who has gone to the Dark Side."

"You think you're an extraordinary being of infinite potential, a match for me? I'm not impressed. In fact, I don't think you're even half as powerful as you think! I'll back up my words."

"Anami, just kill him, I'm late for a dinner date!" Wench-Desiree told him.

"You heard the Wench-----enough talk!" Anami insisted, tired of trading insults.

The GER made his move. He tapped his staff. The

power orb at the tip glowed purple with black streaks encircling it. Anami adorned himself in the black armored body suit; it too had an energy crystal in the headset that glowed white. As the beam from the staff ejected halfway to Anami, it suddenly decelerates to almost stop. Everyone except Anami moved in slow motion. Anami utilized a space-time distortion device built into the suit. Then he moved freely around the energy discharge from the orb of the GER's staff. Anami walked up to the GER, then switched off the time distortion field.

Looking eye-to-eye, Anami with an energy glased from his headset, like a sword, chopped off the head of the GER. A bright purple light enveloped the GER. The GER bellowed a hideous shriek. His staff orb exploded. Purple and black light came out the GER's mouth and eyes. He disintegrated, and was reduced to his fitful black hooded robe and a pile of smoking ashes.

"It is done." Emperor Vox said with a nod.
"When I was a child, my parents used to scare me into being good by telling me that the Grand Exalted Ruler of Chud would get me if I didn't behave. Now I can tell my children that I saw him put to death" Premosee said.
"Can I go now?" Wench-Desiree asked.
"Yes, thanks for your support, and enjoy your dinner date," he said then she beamed up to her ship.

"What an unlucky creature her date will be," Premosee said, then they beamed back to their ships.

A KNOCK AT THE DOOR

Kore sat in the Captain's chair, when suddenly the ship was rocked by the collision of a hull section from an exploded Throx Cruiser.

> "Watch where you're going!" Kore demanded.
> "We're under attack by Knox Warships!" Comdr. Mar yelled. They appeared out of nowhere and fired on our ships. We're surrounded. The shields won't take another blast."
> "Open a channel: Knox Leader, you have no interest in this conflict, cease to interfere with our right to annex this sector of the solar system." Kore told him.

The Knox General appeared on the view screen. He was tall and slim. He had transparent skin. His vital organs were visible. What appeared to be his heart was located in his head, and caused his head to throb. He spoke without moving his lips.

> "You may not agree with our prices and policies; but you don't murder kill our citizens and get away with it. You attacked our Space Station and killed our technicians. Under our laws, we have the right to compensation. We exercise that right. Prepare to be boarded!"
> "What do you want as fair compensation?"
> "Your lives."

The Knox General cut the transmission; he had nothing else to say. His orders were clear: Bring them in to face the Courts or Destroy them all.

> "Warp 8; let's get out of here," Kore ordered.

The Knox bombarded the Throx Cruisers. The Knox weapons were plasma clouds that clung to the Throx vessels, then exploded. All the Throxs Cruisers were targeted. Kore and the entire Armada perished.

The Knox left the vicinity of Earth and returned to their territory.

"I told you the sun would come up!" The Uridian child told the President."
"So you knew the ships weren't Throxs?"
"Yes, I noticed their formation and knew they were Knox Vessels. Why they came to help I don't know. But I do know they're not trouble-makers like Kore, and they likely came to help you and not Alien Kore."

Later at NORAD, President Kensington met with Anami Kordova.

"The invasion is over; Now it's time to rebuild our lives and our cities. We would never have seen this outcome without the help of the Centaurians and the Knox. We owe both of you a debt of gratitude. I also offer my condolence concerning the death of your brother. I know you wanted to capture him alive."
"Kore surrendering wasn't meant to be."
"Are the Knox a friendly bunch?"
"Yes---but as I have been informed---Kore attacked their Space Station to use their Space Bridge without paying or being recorded; so they followed him to Earth to avenge their fallen comrades."

"We have a saying: "The enemy of my enemy is my friend," Pres. Kensington told him.

"Yes, the Knox attack on Kore stopped Kore from attacking you; and while the Throxs attacked you, the Domain was unprotected and we attacked, wiped out the Symbios and killed the GER. What a universe we live in,"

"Right now, Mr. President, our concern is all those guns on the streets!" Gen. West interjected.

"I thought of that before I gave the order to arm the citizens. I believe it was one of the best decisions I've ever made. The civilians killed thousands of Throxs. They freed the military to concentrate on the Cyber-Oz, Throx Cruisers and T-105 Interceptors. Here's what we'll do---we'll buy back the guns. Until then, I believe the criminals have more to fear than the law-abiding citizens."

"Well, I have an Empire to govern. You have my phone number if you need anything."

"You mean Gate Address," Gen. West corrected.

"No, Scientist Chikere developed a video conference system that's tied into your Space Bridge without the Bridge being activated. She's a family-oriented person, and thought it would be great for our governments and citizens to communicate back and forth."

"Centaurus will truly be a long distance call," Gen. West added.